First published in Great Britain in 2016
by Two Blondes Walking Limited

twoblondeswalking.com

Text copyright © 2016 Fi Darby
Illustrations copyright © 2016 Steve Cobbin
Contour representation copyright © 2016 Ordnance Survey
Design by Simon Darby

The author and illustrator have
asserted their moral rights.

ISBN 978-0-9931057-3-9 (Paperback)

The non-story of Ignatious Bowerman

Fi Darby

Illustrations by Steve Cobbin

For my Uncle Tom Cobley

Love from

Fi Darby

Steve Colt

One
Creeping Out

Creeping out of the house was easy; it was the first time I'd done it, but it was still easy.

Outside was cold and a bit misty. As well as being cold and a bit misty, everything looked greyer than normal, because it was twilight, just after dawn (5.50am) and just before sunrise (6.32am).

*(Dawn and sunrise are **not** the same thing. Dawn is when the sky starts to get light, and sunrise is when you first see the sun on the horizon. The correct name for the time between dawn and sunrise is twilight).*

My name is Thomas, I'm eleven years, six months and fourteen days old and I'm extra-ordinary.

I wasn't scared about being out on my own early in the morning; I wasn't scared because I'm extra-ordinary, and I can't do imagining. I think it must be imagining that makes ordinary people scared.

Ordinary people must see things that are actually safe, and imagine that they are unsafe. For example, on a *dimpsy* morning, they might imagine the dark shadow of a tall, man-shaped rock on Dartmoor might really be a forgetful hunter out hunting. I wouldn't imagine this because I'm extra-ordinary, and I can't do imagining.

(Dimpsy means almost dark, but it doesn't mean that if you don't live in Devon).

I expect I need to explain. I often do. Mum says my brain works too quickly for other people to keep up. She's probably right, but she's not a scientist. I am going to be a scientist, and I have a theory. Here it is.

My brain doesn't waste time imagining, which means my neuro-transmitters aren't as distracted as ordinary people's, which means I can think very quickly.

I've decided not to tell Mum my theory; I love her, but she is ordinary.

Now you might think I'm writing a story, but I'm not; these words are about things that actually happened. This is my non-story. I know it's a non-story because:

1. I was there when the things actually happened.
2. I can't do imagining.

As I walked up the drive that dimpsy morning, I saw some odd grey shapes, but didn't imagine they were something else. I walked past a grey car shape with windows, and then some grey sheep shapes with eyes. When I got to the end of the drive, I could see a grey Ignatius Bowerman shape.

(This first time that I crept out of my house, I didn't know his name was Ignatius Bowerman, I just thought he was a tall man-shaped rock).

If I could do imagining, I might have imagined a talking-slash-moving rock called Ignatius Bowerman, and I might have imagined his lost hounds. If I had imagined them, I might have written them down in a story; but I didn't do these things, because I'm extra-ordinary and I can't do imagining.

We had been living in the house on Dartmoor, for six months, one week and three days, when I first noticed that Ignatius Bowerman *(the tall, man-shaped rock)* wasn't there. I noticed it at 5.55am, by looking out of my bedroom window. If you think being accurate about the number of days and the time is extra-ordinary, then you're wrong. I have a calendar on my bedroom wall, as well as a periodic table, and I have an adventure watch with a camouflage strap on my wrist, and I look at all of them. You might have these things; but I don't know, because I don't know you.

On this day, six months, one week and three days after we'd moved to Dartmoor, Ignatius Bowerman *(though I didn't know his name then)* wasn't there when I looked out of my bedroom window.

You're probably going to ask how I could be

sure that he wasn't there. Here's my answer: I used my eyes to check. I'm good at looking; I can look at things for much longer than ordinary people. For example, I once looked at some moss on a gate for twenty-one minutes. It was Hair Moss, but it didn't look like hair.

(I'm not going to tell you any more about Hair Moss here, because I don't think you'll be interested).

I didn't go outside to find out where Ignatius Bowerman *(the tall man-shaped rock)* was, the first morning that I saw him **not** being there; I waited until a day that he **was** there, and went out then. So, six months, two weeks and five days after we moved to Devon, I crept out of my house at 5.59am.

I've already told you that creeping out of my house was easy. Walking up the drive was easy too, except I put my right foot into a puddle; the puddle was approximately ten centimetres deep. My trainers are approximately five centimetres deep, so I got the bottom of my right striped pyjama leg wet. Crossing the lane at the end of the drive was also easy; the lane is one kilometre long.

(One kilometre is the same as one thousand metres).

The lane has a gate at both ends. When we go out in the car, it's my job to open and shut the gates, so Mum can drive through. There were no cars in the lane that night because:

1. It was very early in the morning.
2. Our house is the only house in the lane, and our car was in the drive.

Walking across the moorland to Ignatius Bowerman was not so easy. It took me a longer time than walking up the drive and crossing the lane because:

1. There were gorse bushes.
2. There were big rocks.
3. It was uphill.

Because of the steepness of the hill, I couldn't see Ignatius Bowerman from under the peak of my baseball cap. So I turned my cap round, to make the peak point backwards. It felt a bit strange like that, because I could feel the peak on my neck if I looked up the hill. I didn't look up the hill very often, because there were so many gorse bushes.

It took me eleven minutes to get to where Ignatius Bowerman was; when I got there I wasn't cold any more.

(This was because walking uphill is exercising. When you exercise, your muscles burn fats and carbohydrates. (I'm not going to tell you which muscles; I don't think you'll be interested). When things burn, they heat themselves up and the things next to them. Blood is next to your muscles, so your blood gets warm too, and then moves the warmth all round your body).

The rock *(that was actually Ignatius Bowerman)* wasn't warm, but cold. I knew that, because the first thing I did when I got there was touch him with my hands. I hadn't found out his name yet, but I had found out two things:

1. He was there.
2. He was cold.

The second thing I did when I got there, was walk round the rock *(that was actually Ignatius Bowerman)* and touch him some more. This was difficult because the stones near him were big, and I had to climb over some of them. He was cold all the way round, and a bit wet. That he was cold and wet was not a surprise because:

1. Rocks are mostly cold. *(Some rocks are molten, but then they're usually over 700° centigrade and not touchable by human hands)*
2. It was a bit misty; mist makes things wet because it is drops of water in the air.

When the rock *(that was actually Ignatius Bowerman)* spoke to me, it was a surprise, because I know a lot about rocks, and I know rocks don't usually speak. My counsellor asked me once, if the first thing that Ignatius Bowerman said, was the thing I expected him to say. I didn't answer my counsellor's question, because it was a silly one. Ignatius Bowerman couldn't have said what I expected him to say, because I didn't expect a rock to say anything at all.

If I **had** been expecting a rock to say something, I wouldn't have been surprised about what Ignatius Bowerman said. This is because the first thing that Ignatius Bowerman said was sensible. You people who can do imagining might think a talking rock would say, "Ho, ho, ho." or "Abracadabra." You'd think that, because you'd be mixing a talking rock up with Father Christmas or with a wizard.

(Wizards and Father Christmas aren't real, but Ignatius Bowerman the talking rock is).

Ignatius Bowerman didn't say either of those things.

What he said was, "Hello."

I'm sure you'll agree, person reading my non-story, that 'Hello' was a very sensible thing for him to say. 'Hello' is what people say when they first meet someone. I decided to say something sensible back.

I said, "Hello".

And then we had our first conversation.

Ignatius Bowerman said, "Where have you come from?"

I said, "I came from my bedroom."

Ignatius Bowerman said, "I had a bedroom once."

I said, "Where was your bedroom?"

Ignatius Bowerman said, "It was in my father's house."

I **answered**, "My bedroom's not in my father's house, because my father lives in a prison, not in a house."

By the way, person reading my non-story, I used the word 'answered' then, because I had already used the word 'said' six times in that conversation.

(My English teacher, Mrs. Aitken, told me not to use 'said' too many times. I'm not sure why).

I asked Ignatius Bowerman another question. I asked it, because I wanted to find out why a rock that should have been in a certain place, was sometimes not in that place.

"Where do you go, when you're not here?"

"When I'm not here, I go to search for my lost hounds."

I hadn't met anyone who had lost some hounds before, so I asked, "When did you lose your hounds?"

And he replied, "I lost them three hundred years ago, and I still miss them."

I understood that. I can't do imagining, but I can do feelings. For example, I still miss my dog *(whose name was 'Dog')* and he died two years, nine months and five days ago. Mum said she'd buy me another dog, but I don't want another one. When Dog died, it made me sad. I thought that Ignatius Bowerman was probably sad about missing his hounds; and when I thought that thought, I decided to help him to find them. This meant that I'd need to do an investigation, which was good news, because I'm very good at investigating.

I started the investigation by saying, "I used to have a dog…" and continued it by asking, "… are hounds the same as dogs?"

"My hounds were bigger and fiercer than your dog," replied Ignatius Bowerman.

"You don't know how big and fierce my dog was."

"I do not; but I am very tall and you are very small. I am certain that my hounds would have been bigger and fiercer than your dog."

This made sense, so I believed that Ignatius

Bowerman's hounds were bigger than Dog had been; but this still didn't mean that they would have been **necessarily** fiercer.

So I said, "Some very small dogs are fierce."

This was a true thing to say. Granny used to have a tiny dog named Jim, which sat on her lap, and growled at anybody who wanted to kiss her.

(It never growled at me, mainly because Granny had a whiskery chin and I didn't want to kiss her).

Ignatius Bowerman was insistent.

"There've never been any dogs or hounds as fierce as my hounds."

(Insistent means that you keep saying the same thing over and over again; Mum says that I'm insistent.)

I didn't think that Ignatius Bowerman should have said, 'never'; because 'never' is an infinite amount of time that goes forward forever, and goes backward forever. But I didn't want to disagree with him because:

1. Ignatius Bowerman might have been an infinite age.
2. I wanted to carry on asking him questions.

So I asked this, "What's the difference between a hound and a dog?"

Ignatius Bowerman replied, "Hounds are trained for hunting, they have to be brave and loyal. Was your dog brave and loyal?"

This question seemed like a sensible one, so I thought about it for nine seconds.

"My dog was loyal…"

(I knew Dog was loyal, because he always followed me around).

"…but he was scared of water, so he couldn't have been that brave." Dog hadn't been scared of the water that was in his drinking bowl; but he had been scared of the water in rivers or ponds or streams.

"Well, he wasn't a hound then. My hounds would run through any water and up any hill," said Ignatius Bowerman.

"I used to carry my dog across streams. What if the water was deeper than your hounds?"

"Then they would swim."

I couldn't think of any more questions about hounds, so I stopped asking, and looked at

Ignatius Bowerman instead *(though I still didn't know his name)*. I suspected that I was looking at the back of him. Most rocks don't have a front and a back. But I thought that, as Ignatius Bowerman was talking, he must have a mouth, which would probably be at his front.

I don't know about rocks, but we humans need mouths to form sounds, we use our lips, teeth, tongue and the roof of our mouths. It seemed likely that rocks needed mouths to form sounds too, even though they don't usually speak.

"Where's your mouth?" I asked. Ignatius Bowerman laughed, and I thought two things:

1. That I'd never heard a rock laugh before.
2. That he shouldn't have laughed, because I had asked a sensible question.

After he had finished laughing, Ignatius Bowerman replied, "Walk around me, see where you think my mouth is."

This seemed like a sensible suggestion, but I had no idea what a rock's mouth would look like. I took three steps backwards, so that I could see the top of Ignatius Bowerman, and climbed over the rocks around him in a wider circle than last time.

"I don't know where your mouth is. What does it look like?"

"It looked like a mouth, last time I saw it. But that was three hundred years ago."

I walked round Ignatius Bowerman two more times. I couldn't see a mouth, but there was a shape that I recognised, on what would have been his head, if he was a person. The shape was the shape of a hat with three corners.

"I think I've found the front of you, are you wearing a hat?"

"Oh, I'd forgotten about that," said Ignatius Bowerman, "that's my favourite hunting hat."

"It's a very strange hunting hat. Hats aren't usually made of rock."

"Young man, calling somebody's hat 'strange' is not good manners. Especially when that person's older than you."

Ignatius Bowerman sounded grumpy when he said this.

"I'm sorry, I'm not very good at manners,

because they're difficult to understand; it's because I'm extra-ordinary."

Ignatius Bowerman made a grumpy sound that was a bit like a horse and a bit like an elephant.

"I'm not very good at understanding noises, either," I said.

Ignatius Bowerman made the same grumpy sound again; but this time I was looking at the place under the edge of his cap, where his face was supposed to be, and thought I saw something move.

"Make that noise again, please." *(Mum taught me to say 'please', when I was asking somebody to do something).*

Ignatius Bowerman was still grumpy, "You just asked me to speak to you properly."

"Yes I did, but now I'm asking you to make noises. I think I saw your mouth move, and if you make the noise again, I might find out where your mouth is."

This was the first time I'd ever argued with a rock.

"Watch my lips," said Ignatius Bowerman and let out a very loud horse-slash-elephant noise. I thought two things:

1. I could see Ignatius Bowerman's mouth moving.
2. Rocks don't usually have mouths.

"I can see where your mouth is now. It looks like a crack in a rock," I told Ignatius Bowerman.

*(I've used the word 'told' here, because I'm trying very hard **not** to use the word 'said'; then Mrs. Aitken will like my non-story).*

"Not much good for kissing, then," said Ignatius Bowerman. "I used to like kissing; lots of girls wanted to kiss me, you know."

I didn't know and I didn't want to talk about kissing. The boys at school talk about it, but I don't join in, because it isn't a sensible thing to talk about. I prefer to talk about rocks.

I thought of another question for Ignatius Bowerman, "What's your name?"

I didn't know whether or not he had a name, but I thought he might do, because he was talking to me, and most things that can talk have names.

"My name is Ignatius Bowerman," replied Ignatius Bowerman.

I'd never heard the name 'Ignatius' before. It sounded a bit like 'igneous', which was a coincidence, because 'igneous' is actually the type of rock that Ignatius Bowerman was made of.

(Igneous rock is formed when molten underground rock turns to solid rock (I've already told you how hot molten rock is). Igneous rocks can have crystals inside, but not fossils. All the animals that would have become fossils would have melted instead.)

I know about this for two reasons:

1. I listen in my geography lessons *(most people don't listen in geography lessons)*.
2. I like reading about rocks on the internet.

"Are you sure your name isn't 'Igneous'?" I asked Ignatius Bowerman.

"Of course I am. What a ridiculous suggestion, everybody knows what their own name is."

I thought about this for seven seconds; he was probably right, I couldn't think of anyone who didn't know their own name. Apart from babies, of course, but there are lots of things that babies don't know. I didn't say anything, but Ignatius Bowerman did. I think he might have been grumpy again.

"When someone's just told you their name, it's polite to tell them what your name is."

"Oh, I'm sorry."

I'm often 'sorry' about politeness. Politeness means understanding the rules about what you should be saying. Sometimes what you should be saying is a thing that isn't even true.

(Like when you have to tell your aunty she looks lovely; when what is actually true is, that she has an orange line of make-up all round the edge of her face).

Ordinary people are very sensitive about politeness rules, but I'm not, because I don't think they make sense.

Ignatius Bowerman spoke again, "So, do you have a name, or shall I give you one?"

"No, thank you, I don't need another name, my name is Thomas."

"Thomas is a good name. If you hadn't had one, I'd have called you 'Rocky', which is also a good name."

I didn't think 'Rocky' was a very good name for a boy. I didn't think this for two reasons

1. I had never met a boy called 'Rocky'.

2. I was a person, not a rock.

"Why would you have called me 'Rocky'?" I asked.

"Because 'Rocky' was the name of my smallest hound, and you're very small. It would have been a compliment. Can I call you 'Tom'? I had a friend called 'Tom' once."

"Please don't call me Tom, I don't like it when people shorten names. My name's Thomas, you can call me that. I'll call you Mr. Bowerman."

Ignatius Bowerman didn't say anything, so I asked him another question.

"Do you miss Rocky as much as your other hounds?"

Ignatius Bowerman's rock-mouth moved into a different shape, "I miss Rocky the most. He couldn't run as fast as the other hounds, so he always stayed near to me. He was good company."

I thought about Ignatius Bowerman and his lost hounds for nineteen seconds. After nineteen seconds, I decided to tell him about my investigation decision.

"I'd like to help you to find your hounds."

"I've been looking for them for three hundred years, Thomas." *(It was the first time that any rock had ever said my name).* "What makes you think you can help?"

"I think I can help, because I'm extra-ordinary. I have skills that are useful for investigations. I'm good at thinking, because I don't waste time imagining, and I can look at things for much longer than ordinary people."

"You do indeed sound extra-ordinary, I'd be very grateful for some help. I'd very much like to find my hounds, shall we start now?"

I looked at my green adventure watch with the camouflage strap.

"No, I can't help now, because the time is 6.24am. I have to go to school today, because it's Wednesday."

"In that case, you'd better get back to your bedroom, and get ready for school; learning is important for you youngsters. Which way do you need to go?"

I thought for the first time then, that perhaps Ignatius Bowerman was not very good at looking. I thought this for two reasons:

1. He could see my bedroom window from where he was standing.
2. He'd been looking for his hounds for three hundred years, and still hadn't found them.

I pointed towards my house with my right index finger.

(I chose that finger because index means 'indicate', which is the same thing as pointing).

"It's that way."

"Right then, Thomas. I'll see you again soon, I hope. Come and find me anytime."

I thought about what he'd said.

"Sometimes you go off to look for your hounds; how'll I know when I can find you? I'm very good at finding, but even I can't find a rock that isn't there."

"I'll stay right here until you come back."

"Okay, Ignatius Bowerman, I'll come and see you in forty-eight hours. I may be two or three minutes late."

"Goodbye, Thomas. I have one request."

"Goodbye, Ignatius Bowerman. What's the request?"

"Please could you face me, next time you're talking to me?"

"I am facing you, Ignatius Bowerman. Can't you see my mouth?"

"I'm not looking at your mouth, I'm looking at your cap. If you're facing me, then why is your cap pointing to your back?"

Ignatius Bowerman was obviously confused, I didn't know before that that rocks could be confused. My investigation was going well, because in an investigation, you should always find out lots about the person who wants you to do the investigating *(I learnt this by watching investigation programs on TV).*

Now I knew four things about Ignatius Bowerman:
1. He was a moving rock.
2. He was a talking rock.
3. He wasn't very good at looking.
4. He sometimes got confused.

"A lot of people wear their caps like this," I replied. This was true, when we went on a geography trip to the beach, eleven out of thirteen boys in my class wore their baseball caps with the peaks at the back.

"That is confusing. Please could you wear your cap the right way round next time?"

I turned my baseball cap around. "Yes I can. Goodbye again, Ignatius Bowerman."

Then I walked home, which was quite easy. The big rocks and gorse were still there, but I was getting better at avoiding them. I remembered where the puddle was and I didn't get my right striped pyjama leg wet.

And so the day that was six months, two weeks and five days after we moved to Devon, was the first time for lots of things:

1. It was the first time I'd crept out of my house early in the morning.
2. It was the first time I'd stepped in a puddle in my pyjamas.
3. It was the first time I'd walked on Dartmoor on my own.
4. It was the first time I'd had a conversation with a talking rock.

Two
An Investigation

The next time I crept out of my house was exactly forty-eight hours after the first time that I had said 'goodbye' to Ignatius Bowerman. People don't usually say 'goodbye' to rocks, but I had, because he'd said 'goodbye' to me first.

Creeping out of my house was still easy, and although it wasn't foggy or misty, it was grey again. *(This weather information will be important later in my non-story).* As I left the house through the back door, I didn't worry whether Ignatius Bowerman would be there or not because:

1. He had said, "I will stay here until you return."
2. I could see him from my bedroom window.
3. I don't do worrying.

I didn't step in the puddle that had got my striped pyjama leg wet last time. I took my baseball cap off to walk up the hill, because I couldn't see Ignatius Bowerman through its peak. I could have turned it round, like I had last time, but I didn't want to confuse Ignatius Bowerman about which side of me was the front.

When I reached Ignatius Bowerman, I put my cap on the right way round, and I touched him on his side. He was still cold but not wet this time. I thought that he felt me touch him. I thought this for two reasons:

1. He moved a little bit. The movement was sort of like a shrug, but smaller.
2. He said something to me.

He said, "Hello Thomas."

Ignatius Bowerman had said 'hello' to me

before, and he had said 'Thomas' to me before but he hadn't said 'hello' and 'Thomas' together. So that morning was the first morning that Ignatius Bowerman said 'hello Thomas' to me. It wasn't the last time that he did it.

I replied, "Hello, Mr Bowerman," because that is the correct thing to say if you're talking to a rock, or a grown-up called Ignatius Bowerman, who has just said 'hello Thomas' to you. *(Of course, a rock or a grown-up might say, 'hello Zachary', if your name was Zachary).*

Ignatius Bowerman spoke again. "You're lucky to find me here tonight. There's a new moon, and I often go searching for my hounds **on** a new moon."

I wanted to tell Ignatius Bowerman that he couldn't search for his hounds on a new moon because even at its closest to earth, the moon is 225,623 miles away; but I didn't tell him that, because my Mum says that sometimes I need to remember **not** to say things.

What I said was, "I knew you'd be here, Mr Bowerman, because you said you would be, and

I could see you from my bedroom window."

"I had a bedroom once," Ignatius Bowerman sounded wistful.

(I think wistful should be spelt 'wishtful' because it means being sad and wishing that you had something). He'd obviously forgotten that he'd already told me about his bedroom.

"I know, you told me. It was in your father's house."

I concluded two things from what Ignatius Bowerman said about his bedroom.

('Concluded' means the same as deduced, which nearly means the same as decided).

1. He wasn't very good at remembering.
2. Finding the hounds of someone who wasn't good at remembering was going to be difficult.

I am very good at remembering. For example, I can remember that on the day my Mum told me that my Dad was going to prison, she was wearing a different sort of shoe on each foot.

"My apologies," said Ignatius Bowerman. When you've been a rock for three hundred years, it's difficult to remember everything. "Is your cap pointing to the front of your head?"

I put my left hand up to my cap to check, "Yes it is, Mr Bowerman, you asked me to wear it like that."

Ignatius Bowerman bent over at the waist and looked more closely at me. For the first time, I could see his eyes. His right eye was more open than his left; it was a deep and empty socket, with a rock-eyelid protruding above it.

(Protruding means sticking out, some people have belly buttons that protrude. I have seen them on the internet).

The left eye was a crack, a wide line that got thinner as it went around to the side of his face. Both eyes looked like the eyes of an old person *(I'm not really sure why)*. When Ignatius Bowerman bent over at the waist, it was the first time that I had seen him move any part of him except his mouth. Rocks don't have waists but when he bent over, it looked as though he had one. *(Rocks don't usually have mouths or eyes either).*

"You're right, young Thomas. You're wearing

your cap the right way round today and I can see your mouth."

I decided to change the conversation. My reason for creeping out of my bed, was to do an investigation into where Ignatius Bowerman's hounds were; talking about caps and mouths was not going to be helpful for my investigation.

"Mr Bowerman, I'm here to do an investigation about where your hounds are. I'm going to ask you some questions."

"I miss my hounds."

"I know you do, you told me that last time."

"Did I? I must have forgotten. It's easy to forget things when you've been a rock for three hundred years."

I decided to try not to get annoyed about Ignatius Bowerman forgetting things. It doesn't feel very nice when people are annoyed with you. Their eyes move around in a strange way, and they often turn their bodies around so they're not facing you. Instead of doing that, I decided to sit down on a big boulder facing Ignatius Bowerman. The rock was cold through my striped pyjamas, but I already knew that rocks, except molten ones, were cold.

I looked up at Ignatius Bowerman. I had to tip my head right back.

"My first question is when did you last see your hounds?"

"Ah, my beautiful hounds," he said, "I miss them."

I was trying very hard not to be cross, so I smiled and used a patient voice when I said my next thing. *(Patient voices are slower and quieter than normal ones).*

"You've already told me you miss your hounds; please try not to say the same thing more than once. I'm very good at remembering; I'll remember everything that you say. What I actually asked was, 'when did you last see your hounds?'"

Ignatius Bowerman sighed. *(I discovered then that a rock sighing is a very strange noise).*

"I'm sorry Thomas, I'll try not to say things more than once. I last saw my hounds – three hundred years ago."

Three hundred years was a long time to have been looking for anything, let alone a pack of hounds that could run around. This was not good news for my investigation; but I like to be precise.

So I asked, "Was that exactly three hundred years ago today?"

I could see that Ignatius Bowerman was thinking. Please don't ask me to describe what a rock that is thinking looks like, because I'm not very good at describing. However, if you can do imagining, you probably have a picture in your head right now of a thinking rock.

('However' is a word my English teacher told me to use; it means the same as 'but').

Ignatius Bowerman replied, "I don't know, but I get the impression I've been here a long time; it must be at least three hundred years."

"Not **exactly** three hundred years ago, then," I replied, "I'll remember that. What were you doing when you lost your hounds?"

"I was hunting for hares. I was always hunting, I was very good at it and my hounds were the best

34

hounds in Devon. They called me 'Bowerman the Hunter' because my arrows never missed their targets. Nobody in my father's house or my father's village was ever hungry, because I was so good at hunting and brought plenty of food home for the pots."

I didn't want to ask Ignatius Bowerman too much about hunting for hares, or about hunting for any other animal. I'm a vegetarian, which means I don't eat any meat. I do eat eggs and milk, because they come out of animals that aren't dead. I've done some research about dead bodies, because I want to be a forensic scientist one day. Dead bodies are eaten first by fungi and bacteria, then by fly maggots *(they like the fluids that come out of the dead body)* and then by beetles *(beetles come when the body has dried up a bit)*. I don't eat meat because I don't want to eat fungi *(I don't like mushrooms either)*, bacteria *(I don't like yoghurt either)*, fly maggots or beetles. I also don't want to eat something that's dead.

Even though I didn't want to talk about hunting, I still wanted to help Ignatius

Bowerman, so I asked him a question that was not about hunting.

"Did your hounds have names?"

I already knew that one of the hounds was called 'Rocky', because Ignatius Bowerman had told me this the first time that I'd crept out of my house.

"They all had very important names. They were the strong sixth sons, of strong sixth sons, and were named after the places that they were born; King, Lustleigh, Grim, Bovey, Raven and Hunter."

"What about Rocky?"

"Rocky was different. I found him under a rock on Easdon Down when he was a pup; he was just sitting there, looking lost, and waiting to be found. Rocky wasn't ever very good at hunting; he always stayed with me when the other hounds were chasing hares."

I knew that 'pup' meant the same thing as puppy. Dog had been a puppy when he had first lived with us, but I hadn't named him 'Puppy' because I'd known that he would grow into a dog.

"Was Rocky your favourite hound?"

Ignatius Bowerman looked serious. *(I didn't know before then that rocks could do this).*

"Hunters shouldn't have favourites; but Rocky was my favourite. I couldn't let the rest of the pack see that. They would have killed him. He wasn't as fierce as they were, and they would have been jealous if they'd known how much I loved him. King was the fiercest, he was always in at the kill, but Lustleigh and Grim were the youngest and fastest. Hunter was a bit greedy and sometimes couldn't keep up with the others, Raven and Bovey were the oldest and wisest."

This was good information for my investigation. In my head I was making a table of hound's names and attributes. *(Attributes are things about something; for example, one of my attributes is that I am good at making tables in my head).* Lots of detectives need to write in notebooks to help them to remember things. I'm a bit like a detective, because I do investigations; but I don't need a notebook, because my brain is like a notebook and doesn't forget things.

My brain wrote a table-in-my-head that looked like this.

Hound's Name	Hound's Attribute	Possible Reason for Being Lost
King	Fierce, loyal, always in at the kill	I can't think of a reason
Lustleigh	Fierce, loyal, young, fast	Maybe didn't stop running fast somewhere
Grim	Fierce, loyal, young, fast	Maybe didn't stop running fast somewhere
Bovey	Fierce, loyal, old, wise	Maybe just died of old age
Raven	Fierce, loyal, old, wise	Maybe just died of old age
Hunter	Fierce, loyal, greedy	Maybe someone with lots of food stole him
Rocky	Loyal, bad at hunting	I can't think of a reason

I'm sure that you will agree that this table-in-my-head was:

1. An excellent way of organising information.
2. Going to be very useful for my investigation.

When I'd made the table-in-my-head, *(which took eleven seconds)*, I noticed something strange. The strange thing wasn't about the table-in-my-head, it was about the fact I could see small drips of water running down the front of Ignatius Bowerman. Seeing water when you are outside isn't usually strange. The last time I'd crept out of my house, it had been misty and there had been water everywhere, including on Ignatius Bowerman. This time though *(I told you earlier that this was an important part of the story),* it was grey but not raining or misty and when I'd touched him, Ignatius Bowerman had been dry all over.

Then I noticed something else. Ignatius Bowerman was making a funny noise. He wasn't making the grumpy horse-slash-elephant noise that he had the first time I'd crept out of my house, and he wasn't sighing, he was making a smaller noise that sounded a bit like sniffing.

"Mr Bowerman, why are you making that noise?" I asked, "and why are there drips of water on your front?"

Ignatius Bowerman wriggled and stood up a bit straighter *(I'd never seen a rock wriggle or stand straighter up before, but I thought that was what he was doing)*.

"I'm not making a noise, I'm just telling you about my hounds."

This wasn't true, but I knew that ordinary people sometimes said that they **weren't** doing things when they were really. Once in a while, *(I don't know how long 'a while' is, but my English teacher says that 'once in a while' is a good phrase)*, this means they are crying. Crying is confusing in nearly the same way that politeness is confusing. Mum had told me once; people don't always want other people to know when they are sad. I didn't really understand why, but I concluded that rocks that could **talk** the same as people might do other things the same as people too.

"Okay Mr Bowerman, I won't ask you about that. I won't ask you about the drips of water on your front, either, because you might not want me to know that you are crying."

"There aren't any drips of water, I think you must be seeing things."

This seemed like a really silly thing to say, and I had to try again not to get cross. I wouldn't have known there were drips of water if I hadn't been 'seeing things'. I'd have to have seen them, to know they were there. I decided not to ask questions about the water because:

1. Mum sometimes says I ask too many questions. *(Although she never tells me what the right number of questions is).*
2. Knowing whether or whether not Ignatius Bowerman was crying wasn't going to help my investigation.

I coughed to show that I was changing the subject *(I can't remember how I learnt that people sometimes do that).*

"Let's talk about the investigation; on the

day you lost your hounds, you were hunting for hares. Where exactly were you?"

"It wasn't the day, I was hunting at night."

This was an important piece of information; but I wasn't happy that Ignatius Bowerman hadn't answered the question that I'd meant him to answer.

"Okay, it was night, but where exactly were you?"

"I was hunting on Hayne Down; I'd followed the hounds over from Black Hill. We'd been moving very fast after a large female hare; I'd never seen one so big before, the hounds were very excited and Lustleigh was in the front."

"Where is Hayne Down?"

"I can't remember. I keep looking for it, but so much of the moor looks the same to me now. Rocks, grass, lanes; they're all a muddle in my head. Once upon a time, I knew every boulder, every hare nest."

The bit about the hares sounded wrong and I wondered if Ignatius Bowerman had been doing forgetting again, "Don't hares have burrows and not nests? They aren't birds."

"Rabbits live in burrows, and there are plenty of those round here. They need burrows to hide, because they're slow and live in big families. Hares live on their own, and are so fast, they don't need burrows to hide in; they just run away from danger. Hares are difficult to catch, but I was very good at it."

I'd been noticing for a while now that although Ignatius Bowerman was very bad at remembering some things *(things like what he was wearing and where his hounds were)*, he was very good at remembering the things to do with his hounds and with hunting. This was important information for my investigation; so I made another table-in-my-head that showed what Ignatius Bowerman could and couldn't remember. It looked like this:

Things Ignatius Bowerman Can Remember	Things Ignatius Bowerman Can't Remember
He used to live in a house.	The direction of my house.
His name, my name, his hounds' names.	How long he has been a rock.
What I was wearing (my cap).	What he was wearing (his hat).
The attributes of his hounds.	Where his hounds are.
Facts about hares.	Which things he has already told me.
That he'd been hunting on Hayne Down when he had last seen his hounds.	Where Hayne Down was or is.

This table-in-my-head took twenty-one seconds to make.

You might be wondering, person who is reading my non-story, how I can be so accurate about how long things take. You might be thinking that I was looking at my green adventure watch with the camouflage stripe, when I was making tables in my head; but I wasn't. I just know how long things take. For example, I know it takes an average of fifty-three minutes and five seconds, for my school bus to take me to school. That number is a mean, and I have been to school on the bus ninety-five times now. I could tell you all of the different times that the bus took if you'd like me to, but I don't think you want to hear about that.

At that moment, it was exactly 6.30am. This was an important thing to know because at sometime between 6.45 and 6.52, Mum would come into my bedroom to wake me up *(I'm always awake when she comes anyway, but I pretend to be asleep)*. This was because the day was Friday, and Friday is a school day, except when it is the school holidays. This wasn't the school holidays.

I stood up and looked at Ignatius Bowerman, who'd stopped making sniffing noises.

"I have to go now, Mr Bowerman."

"Oh, that's a shame Thomas. I was enjoying our chat. Where are you going?"

I wasn't sure if Ignatius Bowerman had remembered that I was doing an investigation, and not just having a chat, but I didn't ask him about that.

Instead I answered the question, "First, I'm going back to my bedroom, next I'm going to the bathroom, after that I'm going to the kitchen, and finally I'm going to school. Friday is a school day."

(I used the words 'next', 'after' and 'finally' because Mrs Aitken, my English teacher, told me that it is wrong to use the word 'then' lots of times in the same sentence. I don't know why).

"You must go immediately; learning is important for you youngsters. I didn't do enough learning when I was young, because I was always out hunting. I often wonder now whether having more learning would have helped me to find my hounds."

Ignatius Bowerman had said that learning was important to me before. He was right, learning is very important; I love learning, but I don't love school. At school you're supposed to learn all the time, but it's difficult when only 2.7 people out of a class of twenty-eight want to learn *(this number is an average, you can't have 0.7 of a person, unless that person is dead and chopped up).* Instead of learning by asking important questions the 2.7 people end up being quiet, so that the 25.3 people don't laugh at them and throw pencils at them for wanting to learn. The best learning is definitely learning from the internet. The internet has a lot (probably 94.6%) of the information that you could ever need, and doesn't throw pencils at you. All you need to do is to remember how to find the information. Luckily for me, although I'm sometimes not good at learning at school, I'm very good at finding information on the internet.

I decided then I was going to spend Saturday *(the next day)*, finding information on the internet, to help me with my investigation into the whereabouts of Ignatius Bowerman's hounds. *('Whereabouts' is a long word that's two short words put together. It means 'wheresomethingis').* Ignatius Bowerman had given me some information I could learn more about, and I'd sorted it out in the tables in my head. I knew I wanted to find out:

1. The location of Ignatius Bowerman's father's house.
2. The location of the places that Ignatius Bowerman's hounds had been born.
3. How far Ignatius Bowerman's hounds might have run.
4. Where Hayne Down was.
5. How long Ignatius Bowerman had been a rock.
6. Where Ignatius Bowerman's hounds were.

Question 6 was the most important question; but I knew that I'd have to find the answers to the other questions first.

"Goodbye, Ignatius Bowerman," I said, as I turned to walk back down the hill. "I'll come back soon."

"What time will soon be?" asked Ignatius Bowerman.

"Soon isn't a time, it's a short word that I used instead of saying, 'when I have done some internet research.' I'll probably see you again in two days' time."

"What is 'internet research'?" asked Ignatius Bowerman.

This was a sensible question; and Ignatius Bowerman probably didn't know the answer to it because he was:

1. At least three hundred years old.
2. A hunter who'd probably like hounds and being outside, more than he'd like computers and being inside.

Although the question was sensible, I didn't answer it, because I didn't have time to give the whole answer, and I don't like giving half answers.

So I said, "You probably don't need to understand what 'internet research' is. Goodbye." *(I said 'goodbye' again because I thought Ignatius Bowerman might have forgotten I'd already said it once).*

"Goodbye, Thomas. Thank you for talking to me tonight. I haven't talked to anybody for three hundred years."

It seemed pointless to remind Ignatius Bowerman, the talking rock who often forgets, that he'd talked to me two days ago; so I waved goodbye, and set off down the hill as quickly as I could. I got back into my bed at exactly 6.44am, and Mum came in to wake me up at exactly 6.48am.

Three
Internet Research

On Saturday morning, I started my internet research. I've already told you I like internet research better than school. You might have noticed, person who is reading my non-story, that I've not told you very much about what actually happens when I go to school. I've told you that I listen in geography, I've told you that, on average, only 2.7 people in my classes want to learn, and I've told you I don't always understand why my

English teacher tells me to write things. You may have worked out *(because **you** can do imagining)* that I like Mrs Aitken, my English teacher.

('English' has a capital letter because it is a language, geography isn't a language so it doesn't have a capital letter).

I don't always understand what Mrs Aitken is talking about; but she is a kind person, and tries to help me when the class are writing stories. Stories are a problem for me, because I only like writing about things that are true. That's how you know that the report you're reading now, my non-story about Ignatius Bowerman, is true. I've called it a 'non-story', because it sounds like a story, but is actually true. My mum says, I **always** tell the truth. She's right. For example, when she asked me if I thought her skirt was too short to wear to church last Sunday, I told her that God *(if he existed, which he doesn't, but Mum believes in him)* didn't wear a skirt, so he probably wouldn't know how long they should be. I also told her that her varicose veins looked like blue worms through her tights.

Anyway, I didn't write the last paragraph so I could tell you about English, and telling the truth; I wrote it because I wanted to explain why I haven't told you much about school. As well as it being a difficult place to learn there are four other reasons I don't like school:

1. There are a lot of people at school, and I prefer being on my own *(or with a talking rock)*.

2. I sometimes know more than the teachers *(not Mrs Aitken, though)*. This can make their faces go red, and I don't think they like it.

3. Sometimes I don't understand what teachers are trying to say. Like when a supply teacher thought I wasn't clever and asked me if I was, 'Playing with a full deck', and I told him I thought card games were a waste of time.

4. I don't like pencils being thrown at me, my bag being thrown on the toilet block roof, or being called, 'special'.

I've told you before though, that I do like

finding information on the internet. So, for the rest of this chapter of my non-story, I'll tell you about my internet research into the disappearance of Ignatius Bowerman's hounds. My computer is a laptop. I know a lot of information about my computer; I know its Random Access Memory, its processor speed and one hundred and twenty four other things about it *(I know how many because I've written a numbered list of them, in my blue notebook)*; but I'm not going to tell you all of these things for two reasons:

1. You don't usually see lots of information about computers in stories.
2. People who like computers get called 'geeks'.

My laptop is a good computer, because I can use it anywhere I want to *(apart from sitting on the toilet; Mum tells me off for doing that)*. For this investigation, I put my laptop on my desk, because my desk is next to my bedroom window, and when I sat down at my desk, I could see Ignatius Bowerman, I could also see that it was a sunny day.

Being able to see Ignatius Bowerman was a good thing for two reasons:

1. Seeing him made me want to do my investigation.
2. Seeing him meant I could make sure he was still there.

I was a bit worried about Ignatius Bowerman going places, because I didn't want him to get lost. I thought that him getting lost was possible because he kept forgetting things. For example, the last time I'd crept out of my bedroom *(fifty-three hours and six minutes ago)*, he'd said that when he'd last seen his hounds, they'd been hunting on Hayne Down. He'd also said he didn't remember where Hayne Down was.

I did know where Hayne Down was because on Friday, I'd asked my Mum the question, 'Where's Hayne Down?' The answer had been very interesting; Hayne Down is the hill is straight opposite our house. In fact, Hayne Down is the hill where Ignatius Bowerman was now standing. As I sat at my desk, looking at Ignatius Bowerman, standing on Hayne Down in the sunshine, I decided that this information was important to my investigation for two reasons:

1. If Ignatius Bowerman was on Hayne Down, then his hounds might be there, too.
2. Ignatius Bowerman's memory about places was so bad that he didn't even know where he was.

When I last left Ignatius Bowerman, I had six things I wanted to investigate. My Mum had helped me with number four *(Hayne Down)*, so I still needed to investigate numbers one, two, three, five and six:

1. Where Ignatius Bowerman's father's house was.
2. The names of the places where Ignatius Bowerman's hounds had been born.
3. How far Ignatius Bowerman's hounds might have run.
5. How long Ignatius Bowerman had been a rock?
6. Where were Ignatius Bowerman's hounds?

Number one and number two were about places. A good way to find information about places is on a map. I knew we didn't have a paper map of Dartmoor, because Mum had said, 'I must buy a Dartmoor map, so we can go for some walks', three times since we'd moved to our house. I thought it was likely that there was a map of Dartmoor on the internet, because there are thousands *(I think there might be millions, but I haven't counted them all)* of maps on the internet; there are even maps *of* the internet *on* the internet; so I opened up a Google window and typed the search terms, 'map Dartmoor'.

I hope that you people who are reading my non-story won't call me a 'geek' if I tell you some computer information now; I think you might, so I'll only tell you three facts:

1. When you're using a computer, a 'window' is not something in your bedroom, you can see rocks through; a 'window' is a rectangular part of a computer screen, which shows you different information to another part of a computer screen. *(A*

'window' could be square, because squares are types of rectangles).

2. Google is a company in America that has people who write clever 'sorting information' computer programs called algorithms. *(It also has goats to eat their grass).*

3. A 'search term' is the words you type into Google, to tell Google what information you're looking for. *(I'm very good at search terms).*

When I typed the search term 'map Dartmoor' into the Google program, it took my computer 0.45 seconds to find three useful, and 799,997 not useful, maps *(I'm presuming 799,985 weren't useful, because I only looked at 15 altogether).* The first map Google found was the most useful, so I looked at it very carefully. *(Google algorithms are clever like that).* First, I looked for Hayne Down and my house. When I'd found it, *(which was quite easy because I know that my school bus drives past Haytor twice every school day, and Haytor was easy to find, because it has car parks).* I drew a map-in-my-head, and put my house on it as a red house-shaped symbol. The next thing that I did was look for places near to Hayne Down called: King, Lustleigh, Grim, Raven, Bovey, and Hunter *(the names of Ignatius Bowerman's hounds)*. I found Lustleigh first, because it was in big writing on the map *(big writing on a map means something important)*; Lustleigh is a town *(or village)* and it has a 'PH'.

('PH' means public house, which means pub, which means somewhere that is open to the public, and people drink beer there).

I drew a dog-shaped symbol on the map-in-my-head at Lustleigh. Next, I found 'King' which was actually 'King Tor'. I already knew that a tor is a big, sticking-up lump of rock, because I look at Haytor from the school bus, and I listen *(when other people don't)* in my geography lessons. What I didn't already know, was the thought that I had when I found King Tor on the map. Sometimes my thoughts are like conversations in my head, this was my thought:

"A tor is a sticking-up lump of rock. Ignatius

Bowerman is a sticking-up lump of rock, so, Ignatius Bowerman must be a tor. Ignatius Bowerman can: 1) Move, 2) Talk. So - Tors can 1) Move, 2) Talk."

It would have been quite a long thought for an ordinary person to have, but it was a short thought for an extra-ordinary person like me to have. Being able to have long thoughts that seem like short ones is an important skill for someone who is doing investigations. I drew a dog-shaped symbol next to King Tor on the map-in-my-head. After that, I carried on finding the different places that Ignatius Bowerman's hounds had come from, and drew dog-shaped symbols next to each place on the map-in-my-head. Hunter and Raven were tors quite near to each other and Grim was a place called Grimspound. I found one river called 'Bovey' and two places *(North Bovey and Bovey Tracey)*. I decided to draw the dog-shaped symbol on the map-in-my-head at North Bovey because:

1. Hounds are probably not born in rivers.
2. North Bovey was closest to Hayne Down *(where Ignatius Bowerman was)*.

3. Bovey Tracey sounded like a girl's name, and girls aren't fierce like hounds.

(Except Scarlett Jones in my class, who once bit Jay Parker's ear so hard, blood came out of it).

When I'd finished this part of my investigation, I had one house symbol, six dog-shaped symbols and one man-shaped symbol on the map-in-my-head. The man-shaped symbol was at the place on Hayne Down where Ignatius Bowerman was standing. *(I could see that he was still there out of my bedroom window).* It took me thirty seconds to decide to use a man-shaped symbol for Ignatius Bowerman. I chose a man-shaped symbol because I couldn't decide what a symbol for a talking and moving rock should look like. The map in my head now looked like this:

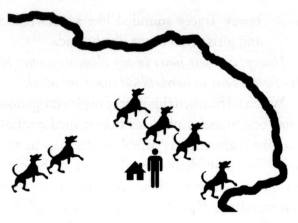

I was pleased with the map in my head, and thought it was useful for my investigation, but I hadn't found everything out. I still needed to investigate numbers one, three, five and six:

1. Where Ignatius Bowerman's father's house was.
3. How far Ignatius Bowerman's hounds might have run.
5. How long Ignatius Bowerman had been a rock.
6. Where Ignatius Bowerman's hounds were.

I decided that the other investigation things

the internet could help me with were things one, three and five. I started off with number one and typed the search question, 'How fast can hounds run?" I want to tell you now, person who is reading my non-story, that one problem with searching for information using Google, is it doesn't always understand exactly what you mean. Even if you type exactly the question you want to ask, the Google algorithms *(computer programs)* have to work out what you're asking, and they sometimes get it wrong. For example, when Scarlett Jones called me 'a complete and utter zero', I asked Google what a zero was, and it showed me a Wikipedia page.

(Wikipedia is an internet encyclopedia that ordinary and extra-ordinary people make up which said, "A zero of a function f is a point x in the domain of the function such that f(x)=0").

You people who are reading my non-story probably don't understand that; I do. But as you can see, Google's answer didn't tell me what Scarlett Jones actually meant when she called me a 'complete and utter zero'.

When I typed my question, 'How fast can hounds run?' Google decided that the word 'hounds' meant the same as the word 'dogs' and showed me 128,000,000 pages of information about fast dogs *(it did this in 0.44 seconds, which was impressive, but it didn't give me the answer to my question)*. One page Google found was about greyhounds, but they didn't look very fierce; Ignatius Bowerman had said all of his hounds were fierce, except Rocky who liked to stay with him. The greyhounds' page said greyhounds are one of the fastest dogs, and can travel sixty-four kilometres in an hour *(there are 1.6 kilometres in one mile)*.

The Dartmoor map-in-my-head shows an area of forty-four square kilometres, which meant that if Ignatius Bowerman's hounds were greyhounds, they would be able to leave my map area in approximately six minutes and nine seconds. *(I said 'approximately' then, because it would depend which direction they were going in).* I represented this information on the map-in-my-head by an arrow. It looked like this:

The information about the speed of Ignatius Bowerman's hounds was a bit useful to my investigation. It was a bit useful because:

1. Now I knew that the hounds could have run a long way from Hayne Down.
2. I suspected if I found them, I wouldn't be able to catch them, because they could run so fast.

Sometimes *(especially when you're using the internet)* the answers to questions can lead to new questions.

(Socrates was a man who asked a lot of questions. He asked so many questions that people (probably ordinary ones) got very annoyed with him and executed him. (I learnt that in a philosophy lesson when I was the only person listening). Keeping on asking and answering new questions like Socrates did, helps you to learn lots of things, but it can take up a lot of time).

I didn't want the internet part of my investigation to take too long, so I decided the next things I needed to find out, were numbers one and five:

1. Where Ignatius Bowerman's house was.
5. How long Ignatius Bowerman had been a rock.

Both of these questions had the words 'Ignatius Bowerman' in them, so I decided to do internet searches using separate search terms 'Ignatius' and 'Bowerman'. When I typed 'Ignatius', Google took 0.49 seconds to find 19,200,000 pages of information. I didn't read all of them, but I did find out one interesting fact – Ignatius means something. Most names have meanings; for example, Thomas means 'twin'. I think my Mum must not know about name meanings, because I haven't got a twin. Ignatius doesn't mean 'twin', it means 'fiery one', which is interesting because I thought Ignatius Bowerman's name should have been 'Igneous', which means rock that was once molten and very hot and fiery.

When I did an internet search using the term 'Bowerman', Google found 838,000 pages in 0.22 seconds *(this was my quickest internet search for this investigation so far)*. The pages weren't:

1. Useful for my investigation.
2. At all interesting.

Sometimes it's just like that with Google. I think I might like to write algorithms one day; I know what's interesting, and I could write an *'Is it interesting enough?'* algorithm, to make sure nobody was ever bored by the information that their searches gave them. Sometimes you can make an internet search more interesting and useful, by adding another word to your search term. I added the word, 'Dartmoor' because I thought that Ignatius Bowerman's hounds were probably still on Dartmoor. When I did this, Google found 17,100 pages of information in 0.37 seconds, and most of those pages had the same, very significant *(significant is a word that Mrs Aitken told me to use instead of 'important')* information. I'm quite excited about telling you this information, because it was the first real breakthrough in my investigation.

(Breakthrough is another long word that is two short words joined together, and it means something that takes you nearer to achieving your goal).

Here is the significant and interesting information – **lots of people already knew about Ignatius Bowerman**.

Except that they didn't know that he was a moving-slash-talking rock named Ignatius Bowerman; they thought he was just a normal rock called 'Bowerman's Nose' or 'Bowerman the Hunter'. The internet pages gave me that significant and interesting information, and they also gave me a story about how Ignatius Bowerman had been turned into a rock *(I'll tell you about that later in my non-story)*. All this meant that Ignatius Bowerman wasn't just a moving-slash-talking rock, he was a legend.

Now, I need to explain the word 'legend' to you very carefully. When people at school try to be show-offs, they sometimes use the word 'legend' to talk about somebody that is really good. The ordinary kids at school think this is great when the people trying to be show-offs say it; but when teachers say 'legend', they think it's weird and embarrassing. When I said Ignatius Bowerman was a 'legend' in my last paragraph, I meant that Ignatius Bowerman was a story. *(A legend is a story that is very old)*. This was great news because:

1. Legends sometimes have information in them that is true.
2. Some of the true information might help me to find Ignatius Bowerman's hounds.

The legend of Bowerman the Hunter was the same on all the fifteen Google pages I read. I've written my version of it for you here, and put stars like this ** where the legend matched what Ignatius Bowerman had said to me, and circles like this °° where the legend matched what I'd noticed about Ignatius Bowerman when I was talking to him.

Once upon a time *(my teacher at primary school used to say that this was a good way to start a story, but Mrs Aitken doesn't like it; I don't know why)*. There was a fine *(another word for good)* hunter called Bowerman **. Bowerman was tall °° and powerful °° and had a pack of fierce hounds **. Bowerman's favourite activity in all the world *(he actually only went to a tiny bit of the world)* was hunting, and he was so good with his bow, and so generous, that all of the people in his village had plenty of food to eat **. One evening, Bowerman was out hunting, when he upset a group of witches *(this is just a story, I'm not saying that witches are real)* by galloping after his six fierce hounds *(and one not so fierce hound **)* through an important Dartmoor witches' meeting. Bowerman didn't like witches, because all of the villagers were afraid of them; so he laughed as he rode through their group, and this made the witches very cross. The witches stayed cross with Bowerman all night, and the next day they hatched a plot. *(This doesn't mean that they sat like chickens on their eggs; it is an idiom that Mrs Aitken taught me. An idiom is a confusing way of writing something in words that don't actually mean that thing).* One witch turned herself into a giant hare **, and waited where she knew that Bowerman and his hounds would be hunting. When Bowerman and his hounds found her, she ran and ran all night. Bowerman and his hounds chased after her until they were exhausted. They ended up on a hill called Hayne Down °°, and all of the hare-slash-witch's friends were waiting for them there. As Bowerman ran towards the witches, they cast a powerful spell and turned Bowerman into a tall rock °°.

I must say to you here, person that is reading my non-story, that I don't usually believe in anything I can't prove *(witches would be an example of this)*. This is because:

1. There is so much provable information in the universe; it would be a waste of time believing in not-provable things.

2. I can't do imagining.

However, *(Mrs Aitken told me to use this word when I give a new opinion)* I'm good at seeing and remembering things that actually happen; and a talking rock was something I'd seen, and something that had actually happened. So I knew that moving and talking rocks were provable *(my eyes proved it)* but I didn't know whether or not witches were provable.

I was fairly sure the legend from the internet was about **my** walking-slash-talking rock, Ignatius Bowerman. It seemed like too much of a coincidence, that so many things in the legend matched what I'd actually seen and heard when I visited him.

(A coincidence is when two things happen at once that look like they're connected, but really aren't).

I thought for thirty seconds, which is a long time for me, about the progress of my investigation. I had two tables and a map-in-my-head; these showed me some interesting and useful information. I also had a legend, which gave some clues about how Ignatius Bowerman became a rock. I didn't think these four things gave me enough information yet to find out where Ignatius Bowerman's hounds were; but they would definitely make it easier. I thought about what I needed to do next, and I decided the most important thing to do, would be to find out if the legend-slash-story about Bowerman the Hunter was actually true *(I thought that it mostly was)*. There was only one way to do that.

I needed to talk to Ignatius Bowerman.

I needed to creep out of my bedroom for a third time.

Four
Eggs with Mum

I decided I'd go and visit Ignatius Bowerman again that night once Mum had gone to bed. Mum and I usually had egg and chips for tea on Saturday night, and then watched TV *(that means television)* together. I sometimes like watching TV, if it isn't too loud and flashy. TV on a Saturday night is often loud and flashy, but I watch it anyway, because Mum says that it is important for families to do things together. I used to think that to be a family, you had to have lots of people; maybe a mum and a dad *(sometimes you can have a mum and a mum, or a dad and a dad, but not very often)* and two or three children; I don't think that now because when my Dad went to prison, Mum said that two of us was still enough to make a family.

I don't really like talking about my Dad going to prison, because I miss him; but I'll tell you that the bad thing he did was steal something. It wasn't a jewel or a watch or anything like that; Dad stole some money from a company that he was working for. I once asked Mum where the money was now, and she said that it wasn't that sort of money. She said that it was money that was moved around between computers. She also told me that the police had taken the money back out of Dad's computer, when they had caught him.

When Dad was stealing the money, we lived in London *(I like the Underground maps in London, they make a lot of sense)*. We moved to Dartmoor *(which is in Devon and 218 miles from London)* because Dad is in a prison in a town called Princetown, which is nearly in the middle of Dartmoor. We are allowed to go and visit Dad once a fortnight, and I usually show him my list of things that I know about computers. Dad looks sad when we visit him, but I think he likes my list.

I don't want to tell you any more about that.

While Mum and I were eating our Saturday egg and chips *(I like to have two fried eggs that aren't touching each other)*, Mum asked me questions about what I'd been doing *(she often does that)*.

She said, "What have you been doing up in your room all day?"

I replied "I've been looking up Dartmoor legends on my computer. There are lots of them, Google found 175,000."

I didn't tell Mum about Ignatius Bowerman because;

1. I didn't want to tell her that I'd been creeping out of the house.
2. I didn't think that she would believe in a walking-slash-talking rock.

"It's not like you to want to read that sort of thing. You're usually more of a facts man."

"I'm not a man, I'm nearly a teenager. And I already know lots of facts about Dartmoor."

Mum laughed, "Okay, Mr. Nearly Teenager, tell me two facts about Dartmoor.

"Well..., " I took 15 seconds to decide which facts Mum would like best, "Did you know that Dartmoor is 368 square miles, which is the same as 954 square kilometres?"

Mum looked as though she liked my first fact. "No, I didn't, I knew it was big, and that it takes two days to walk across from north to south, but 368 square miles is quite impressive."

I made a note in my head that it takes two days to walk across Dartmoor. I did this because I thought that the information might be useful for my investigation.

Mum said, "That's one fact, which other fact are you going to tell me?"

I'd already decided the next fact, "The highest point on Dartmoor is 621 metres above sea level and is called High Willhayes."

"That's quite high, would you like us to walk there one day?"

I thought about this question, I was busy with my investigation and didn't think that Ignatius

Bowerman's hounds were on High Willhayes; but Mum had said, *'one day'* which means *'not today, and I'm not going to decide when'*; which would be okay because by the time we went for the walk, I would probably have finished my investigation and found the hounds.

I replied, "Yes please, but could we go on a sunny day?"

Mum didn't mind going out walking in the wind and rain, but I did. It didn't make sense to go out and get cold and wet, when you knew that in a couple of days it would be fine again.

"We can definitely go on a sunny day. I must buy a Dartmoor map."

That was the fourth time that Mum had said, *'I must buy a Dartmoor map'*, since we'd moved to Devon.

I told her, "There are lots of Dartmoor maps on the internet; I've been looking at where we live. Did you know that the big rock on the hill over there is called, 'Bowerman's Nose'?"

"This house used to be called, *'Bowerman's Cottage'* when I was a girl. I used to come to Dartmoor with my grandparents and we stayed here twice. I'm quite familiar with Mr Bowerman."

This was my second bit of exciting news that day. We lived in 'Bowerman's Cottage'. *(The first exciting thing had been finding out that Ignatius Bowerman was a legend)*. I thought about Mum calling Ignatius Bowerman, **'Mr Bowerman'** and was a little bit suspicious; did she know that Bowerman's Nose was, in fact, a moving-slash-talking rock?

I asked, "Why did you just call the rock *'Mr Bowerman'* and not *'Bowerman's Nose'*?"

"Well, it seemed more polite to me; he's got a big sticking out bit that looks like a nose and I thought he might be sensitive about it."

I was still suspicious after Mum's answer. I was suspicious for two reasons:

1. If it's unusual to talk to rocks, being polite to them must be super-unusual.
2. Rocks are usually called 'it', and Mum kept calling Ignatius Bowerman, 'he'.

I asked Mum a risky question, *(it was risky*

because I didn't want her to guess I'd been talking to a rock).

"Do you think rocks can talk?" One second after I'd asked it, I wished I hadn't.

Mum hesitated before she replied, "Well, I'm not an expert on rocks. All I would say is, Dartmoor is a very old place, where very strange things happen."

I wondered then if Mum had ever crept out of her bedroom, to go and see a talking-slash-moving rock that said, 'Hello, Sarah.' *(Sarah is one of Mum's names).* I wanted to find out more about what Mum had meant when she'd said that 'strange things' happen on Dartmoor; but I didn't think I could ask any more questions without giving away my motives, so I didn't.

(Motives are the reasons that you do things; for example, when my Dad used a computer to steal money from his company, he did it because he wanted to buy a bigger house for us all to live in. Buying a bigger house was his motive).

I wanted to ask Mum a safe question, so she wouldn't guess I'd been talking to a rock.

So I said, "Do you know the legend of Bowerman the Hunter?"

"Granddad used to tell me the story. Those nasty witches! Did you know that most of the evil witches were chased out of Devon, after they were so mean to poor old Bowerman?"

I said, "I don't believe in witches."

Mum laughed, "That's probably because you've never met one. There are still some white witches around Devon; but they're usually nice old ladies who know a lot about making medicines out of herbs and just want to be left alone."

"Do they cast spells on people?"

"Not actual spells, at least I don't think they do. The stories about spells came about, because witches were so good at making medicines and poisons."

"Would I know if I was talking to a witch?"

"Not necessarily, but when you next see an old woman with a pointy hat and a warty nose, you'll probably know she was a witch."

I could tell Mum was teasing me now. There were two reasons that I could tell:

1. Little lines appeared across her cheeks, as she tried not to smile.
2. She winked at me.

Mum and I agreed the winking signal a long time ago. I find it difficult to tell if people are teasing, because I always tell the truth, and teasing is a sort of lying. Mum likes teasing me, but she didn't want me to be upset and not understand that she was teasing; so we agreed she would wink when she was teasing, and not wink, when she was telling the truth. This system works very well, unless Mum has a cold. When she has a cold, she looks like she's winking all of the time.

I decided then it was time to stop asking Mum questions about Ignatius Bowerman, so that she didn't get suspicious about my investigation. Mum being suspicious about my investigation would be bad, because she might guess I was creeping out of my bedroom, and tell me to stop. On Saturdays, when we have had our eggs and chips for tea, it's always my turn to do the washing-up. I don't mind this rule for two reasons:

1. Mum does the washing up all the rest of the time.
2. The loud TV is in the lounge, and the sink is in the kitchen.

I usually take a long time to do the washing-up because I like to make sure everything is perfectly clean. It doesn't take very long to make sure that plates and cutlery are perfectly clean, but the frying pan always has lots of stuck-on brown bits on it; I have to use the green scrubber to get them off. While I'm washing up, Mum goes and sits on the sofa in the lounge, and watches the loud TV. I go and sit with her after I've finished.

On this Saturday night, I didn't want to sit for too long on the sofa, being a family and watching the loud TV, because I wanted to go back to my bedroom and get ready to go and ask Ignatius Bowerman some more investigation questions. I thought that Mum would be disappointed if I went upstairs at eight o'clock, so I waited until ten past eight and told her I was tired. She was so busy watching loud TV, that she didn't seem to mind; so I went upstairs and read twenty more versions of the 'Bowerman's Nose' legend-slash-story on the internet and thought about the map-in-my-head.

*(Maps in general have symbols on them to show important things. My map only had **nine** things on it. All of them were important but I knew that I needed more information).*

At ten thirty, I decided that Mum would be asleep, and that I would be able to creep out of the house without her hearing me. I knew *(because I'd been looking out of my bedroom window)* it was dark enough outside for me to need a torch. I got my wind-up one out of the drawer under my bed. I chose that one, because it's the only torch that I have. I picked up my jacket in the porch and put it on, because it is colder at night-time than it is during the day, and I put my baseball cap on the right way round.

When I got outside I realised three important things:

1.   Mum's bedroom window was open.
2.   I couldn't wind my torch up, because it's

noisy, and she would hear it.

3. I would have to walk up the drive in the dark.

I don't know if you live in a town or in the country; but if you live in a town, you'll be used to it being quite light at night-time. Even if the street lights go out *(they didn't in London)*, there'll be light from houses and cars. At night in our lane on Dartmoor, the only light is the light from the moon and the stars.

(The light from the moon is actually reflected light from the sun).

Except, this Saturday night was cloudy. This meant that:

1. The moon and stars were hidden.
2. I could hardly see my left hand when I held it up in front of my face. *(I didn't hold my right hand up, because I was using it to hold my torch).*

I thought about this problem for sixteen seconds, and came up with quite a good solution.

Our drive has a wooden fence along the left side *(if you're facing the lane)*. If I could hold onto the fence, I could find my way far enough down the drive, to be able to wind my torch up without Mum hearing me. I couldn't see anything, but I wasn't scared at all. I was a bit worried though, that I might not be able to find Ignatius Bowerman *(you'll see later in my non-story, that I was right to be worried about this)*.

Before I could hold on to the fence and walk up the drive, I had to find the fence. I put my torch into my jacket pocket, and put both hands out in front of me. When I was at primary school, some of the boys used to pretend to be mummies and zombies by walking around with their hands out in front of them. I didn't do that because I thought that it was silly.

(Mummies are specially treated dead bodies, which definitely can't walk, and zombies are not even real. I'm particularly interested in mummies because I'm interested in dead bodies. I know lots about them but I'll just tell you this one thing. The only organ left in a mummified body is the heart).

I walked slowly off in what I thought was the direction of the fence. It felt odd walking and not being able to see where I was going, so I took smaller steps than usual *(I guessed they were thirty centimetres each)*. I walked twelve steps before I reached the fence. *(That means I walked three metres and sixty centimetres)*. I knew two steps before I touched the fence that I was nearly there, because I stepped into the mud that runs up the side of the drive. I'd forgotten about that. *(I probably only forget something once a month)*.

(Not very many people know your ability to see in dim light gets better after about ten minutes. This is because of things in your eyes called rods, and a chemical called rhodopsin; but I don't think you want to hear any more about that).

By the time I got to the fence, I could see it, but only the bit just in front of me. I put my left hand onto the top of the fence, turned 90º, and started walking. I could feel my feet getting wet and muddy, and also a bit cold. I stopped and looked towards the lane; I could see fence for two more metres, which meant that, if I walked on the very edge of the drive, next to the mud but not on it, I would still be able to see the fence, and still be able to follow it. This was a great idea and worked very well, except that I trod in the same puddle I'd trodden in when I first crept out of my house to see Ignatius Bowerman. This time, I didn't just get my left striped pyjama leg wet; I got both of my striped pyjama legs wet. It was a cold kind of wet, and I didn't like it.

When I reached the lane, I decided two things:

1. It was going to be impossible to find Ignatius Bowerman without any light.
2. I was far enough from the house to wind up my torch.

So I started winding. Wind up torches are good, because you don't have to find batteries to use them, but they're bad, because they take quite a long time to wind up, and they're loud while you're doing it. It felt a bit strange standing at the end of our drive, making lots of noise in the dark for one minute and twenty seconds; which is how long I could wind for before my arms were aching so much, I had to stop. Once my torch was working, I shone it in front of me and crossed the lane. On the moorland hill that led up to Ignatius Bowerman, I realised how useful my torch was. If I shone it onto the ground, I could make sure I didn't trip over any rocks or gorse bushes. I kept walking up the hill for eleven minutes and then stopped. It was possible that I could walk past Ignatius Bowerman; even tall things can be tricky to see in the dark, if your torch isn't shining right at them. *(I knew I had to stop after eleven minutes because that was how long it took me to get from the lane to Ignatius Bowerman, the first time I visited him).*

I turned round 360° very slowly, moving my torch up and down as I went. *(360° is a whole turn so I ended up facing the same way that I'd started).* I didn't see Ignatius Bowerman, so I turned 360° again in the other direction. I'm not sure why I changed direction. I still couldn't see Ignatius Bowerman; this meant one of two things:

1. I was in the wrong place, in the dark, on Dartmoor.
2. Ignatius Bowerman wasn't there again.

As I didn't know which of those two things

was the right one, I wasn't sure what to next. So I stood there and thought about my dilemma for thirty-five seconds.

(A 'dilemma' is when you have to make a tricky decision that all of the thoughts, and table and maps in your head can't help you with).

After thirty-five seconds, I decided I had three options:

1. Turn another 360° and shine my torch some more.
2. Go back to my bedroom, hide my dirty trainers and go to bed.
3. Walk around and look for Ignatius Bowerman.

I was a bit worried about option three, but I didn't want to do options one or two yet. Option three was a risky option, because if I started wandering around in the dark too much, I might get lost and not be able to find my way back home. I thought for another ten seconds, and came up with a plan. I'd walk around and look for Ignatius Bowerman, but I'd do it in a clever and sensible way. I'd face as straight up the hill as I could in the dark, and walk forward fifteen paces, then I'd shine my torch around. Next, I'd turn 90°, so I was facing right and walk another fifteen paces, then I'd shine my torch around again. If I did this turning-slash-walking-slash-shining thing two more times, then I'd end up back where I started, and I'd have looked for Ignatius Bowerman in quite a big area. My only worry about this plan, was that I wouldn't know if I was turning exactly 90° or not; being on a slope would help me with this, because I'd know if I was facing uphill, downhill, or sideways. A compass was what I really needed, and I made a note-in-my-head, to ask Mum if I could have a one for my birthday on the 8th of August.

I started to do my plan, and walked up the hill for fifteen paces. It was difficult to walk in a straight line because of the rocks and gorse bushes. When I shone my torch, I didn't see anything that looked like a moving-slash-talking rock, so I decided to add 'shouting' to my plan. I chose to shout the words 'Ignatius Bowerman'. I chose these words because:

1. Calling someone's name when you're looking for them is a sensible thing to do, even if that person is a rock.
2. I didn't want to find any other moving-slash-talking rocks on Hayne Down.

Shouting 'Ignatius Bowerman' didn't help me find him, so I turned what I estimated to be 90°.

(An estimate is a guess that you think about carefully before you guess it. I prefer estimating, as guessing is a waste of time).

I'd just counted up to pace nine for the second time, when my torch light went very dim. That's the problem with wind-up torches. They're good for the environment *(because they're powered by arm muscles)* and they're cheap to run *(because you don't have to buy batteries)* but they tend to run out of light, just when you don't want them to. I thought it would be silly walking any further with a really dim torch, so I started to wind again. The winding sounded even louder now that I was up a hill in the dark on my own, than it had when I'd been at the end of my drive in the dark on my own. I didn't really like the noise, so I wound really quickly, to try and make the torch charge up faster. This was a mistake *(I don't very often make mistakes)* because I was winding so hard I dropped the torch. *(Let me tell you this now, person who is reading my non-story, I didn't just drop the torch in a fall-straight-down-to-the-ground way, I dropped it in a fly-into-the-air-and-smash-to-the-ground-on-a-rock way).*

This was bad news *(a phrase that Mrs Aitken told me to use if something had gone wrong in a story)*. It was bad news because:

1. I couldn't see where my torch was.
2. It was really, really dark.
3. For the first time since my investigation had started, I was actually scared.

Five
Figgie Daniel

The physical things that happen when you're scared aren't actually bad. Most of the feelings are to do with your body getting ready to either run away, or fight off something dangerous. My problem with being scared is that it doesn't happen to me very often; this means that it takes me by surprise when it does. I knew that I was scared because:

1. I had a prickly feeling down my back.
2. I didn't want to look behind me.
3. I had a sense of impending doom.

You might be wondering, person who is reading my non-story, what *'a sense of impending doom'* is. I first read about it when I was doing some internet research about forensic science. People often have *'a sense of impending doom'* when they're about to have a heart attack and die. It means that they think that something really bad is going to happen. In the case of a heart attack, they would have been right to have *'a sense of impending doom'*, because dying is just about the worst thing that can happen to a person. In my case *(a teenage boy with a broken torch on a dark moor)* the *'sense of impending doom'* was not really necessary, because what actually happened then – although it was a massive surprise and made me jump – was definitely not as bad as dying.

I've just told you that I didn't want to look behind me. After *'what happened next'* had actually happened, I didn't want to look behind me even more because *'what happened next'* was that a very deep and scary voice, that was close behind me, said something.

The voice said, "What do you want?"

As you can imagine *(because you're not like me, and can do imagining)*, I didn't know what to do next. I'm sure that I thought of all of the possible things to do, but none of them seemed like a good idea. The things were:

1. Run away. This was a bad idea, because I couldn't see the ground or my feet.
2. Turn around. This was a sensible idea, but I couldn't make my body do it.
3. Reply to the voice. I chose this thing, but I don't really know why.

I said, "I want my torch to start working again, and I want you to tell me who you are." Which seemed to me to be a good thing to say, because the voice had asked, 'What do you want?' And those two things actually were what I wanted at that moment.

"My name is Ignatius Bowerman, and you're not carrying a torch."

When I heard that, I turned around so quickly that I nearly fell straight into Ignatius Bowerman. I put my hands against him to steady myself; he felt cold and dry. I was cross about being scared, but I wasn't sure whether I was cross with myself or with Ignatius Bowerman.

"You scared me!"

"I'm sorry, I didn't mean to scare you. Is it because I'm so tall? People used to be scared of my hounds, because they were so fierce, but I don't know where my hounds are anymore. Have you seen them?"

"Mr Bowerman ..." *(I said Mr Bowerman because he was a lot older than me, and because Mum had said that it would be polite)* "... it's Thomas. I've come to help you find your hounds."

"Thomas? Thomas?" Ignatius Bowerman sounded like he was trying very hard to remember. "Ah yes, young Thomas. Last time I saw you, you said that you were going to come back 'soon'. That was two years ago, but well done for remembering to wear your cap the right way round."

"It wasn't two years ago...," I started to say, and then remembered that Ignatius Bowerman could only remember certain things, and that most of them were about his hounds. Instead I asked a question, "Where have you been tonight?"

"I haven't been anywhere tonight," replied Ignatius Bowerman, "I only really like going hunting, and I can't find my hounds."

I didn't know what to say to that. I thought that it was likely that he'd been somewhere, because I hadn't been able to find him, but I could have been looking in the wrong place. I decided not to disagree with him.

"I've come to help you to find your hounds."

"Oh, have you? That is very kind, their names are King, Lustleigh, Grim..."

"... Bovey, Raven and Hunter," I interrupted, "And don't forget Rocky."

"You shouldn't interrupt your elders," said Ignatius Bowerman, "it is bad manners. How do you know my hounds' names? Have you stolen them?"

I was feeling a bit impatient *(this was probably because of the adrenaline that my body had produced when I was scared).*

"No, I haven't stolen your hounds and you told me their names last time I saw you. I remembered because I'm very good at remembering. You didn't remember because you're not very good at remembering."

"Oh, I see. Oh, Thomas, I'm really sorry. I'm a silly old hunter who forgets everything; and you've come to help me."

And with that, Ignatius Bowerman sat down heavily on a rock.

I don't know if you have ever seen a rock sit down heavily on another rock; but if you say that you haven't, you will be in the same position as me. I didn't actually see Ignatius Bowerman sit down, because I'd dropped my torch and it was very dark; but I did hear him sit down. I discovered that night, that a sitting-down rock makes a slow creaking and grinding sound, and then, if the sitting down is happening onto another rock, there is exactly the same noise that you hear when you bang two stones together.

(This is not, by the way, the same sound that you hear when you bang two people's heads together. I know this because I did it to Sam Arnold and Sam Ricketts when they threw my school bag on the toilet roof).

I decided next that I should stop looking for

my torch, and concentrate on my investigation. I felt around with my hands for a big enough rock and sat down on it, facing where I thought Ignatius Bowerman was.

"Please can I ask you some more questions about your missing hounds?"

"You certainly can, their names are King, Lustleigh..."

"Sorry to interrupt again, Mr Bowerman, but you've already told me their names. Can I ask you about the witches?"

"You do know that interrupting is rude, don't you, Thomas?" said Ignatius Bowerman, but he didn't sound cross. "You can ask me about the witches, but I won't be able to tell you anything good about them. I hate witches."

I wasn't surprised by this information; if I was a hunter that had been turned into a rock by witches, I'd probably hate them as well.

"Do you mind me asking why you hate witches?" I asked.

"Not at all, ask away," replied Ignatius Bowerman.

This wasn't the answer that I'd expected. I'd thought that he would tell me about being changed into a rock. I tried asking in another way. *(I sometimes have to do that with ordinary people who don't understand what I'm talking about).*

"Why do you hate witches?"

That got a more useful response. "I hate the hags, because it's their fault that I've been a rock for three hundred years, and it is their fault that I've lost my hounds."

(I should tell you here that 'hags' is another word for witches).

"Why is it the witches' fault that you have been a rock for three hundred years?" I already knew the answer to that, but I wanted to hear what Ignatius Bowerman had to say.

"Because it was those old hags that turned me into a rock. They used their spells and mumblings to do it; just because I rode through one of their horrible meetings and knocked their cauldron over."

This explanation made me feel sorry for

Ignatius Bowerman, but it made me feel happy for my investigation. Being sure of things in an investigation is very useful; and I was now sure that Bowerman the Hunter from the legend of Bowerman's Nose, was the same rock-slash-person as the Ignatius Bowerman who was sitting *(somewhere)* in front of me. This was great information, but it didn't tell me where the hounds were. I needed to ask some more questions.

So I asked, "Why is it the witches' fault that you have lost your hounds?"

"Thomas, what would you feel like, if you saw someone that you loved being turned into a rock?"

I thought about this for eight seconds. The only people that I loved were my Mum and Dad. I liked Mrs Aitken a lot, but people don't love teachers.

"Well, nobody I love has ever been turned into a rock; but when my Dad was sent to prison, I felt very sad and I worried I wouldn't see him again."

"My hounds loved me and I think they must have been sad and worried, too. You must understand that being turned into a rock was not instant. The witches' spell worked slowly; first it stopped me from moving, then my feet changed into rock, and next my ankles. It hurt and I was very angry, so I shouted at the witches, I used bad words that I don't usually use. When I realised I'd turned into rock right up to my waist, I'm ashamed to say that I became frightened, and started to scream at the witches. My hounds could smell that I was frightened and that made them frightened too. Raven ran away first, and the others followed him. All of my beautiful hounds gone, except Rocky. Rocky stayed with me like he always did; he wasn't very clever, and hadn't worked out what was happening. The last thing I saw as my eyes hardened was Rocky looking up at me."

I didn't know what to say about the witches. As well as losing his hounds, Ignatius Bowerman had been through a very horrible experience. I waited for forty seconds, and then asked my next question.

"Where do you think your hounds might have run away to?"

"At first I thought they would run straight to my father's house. That was their home, and they all knew how to get there. After the witches had gone, I tried to get there, but I couldn't move or see. It took me a month to learn how to open my eyes and a year to move again. I could feel Rocky lying right next to me, but I couldn't even speak to him."

"Where was your father's house?"

"I'm a silly old hunter, I can't remember where it was."

"Can you remember anything about what it looked like?" I asked this question, because I thought if I had a description of the house, I might be able to find it myself.

"I can remember it had trees on one side, and a long hill behind it."

This wasn't very much information, but I made a note-in-my-head to look for a place on the Dartmoor map on the internet that fitted the house description. I decided to ask some questions that might give me a different type of information about the house.

"What was it like living at your father's house?"

"It was a good life. My father was very strict but he was a fair man. My mother died when I was four, but that didn't stop the house being a busy one. We always had visitors; they were usually hunters, who wanted to try out their skills on Dartmoor. When we were young, my brother and I used to sit on the stairs, and watch them laughing and drinking with my father after a long day out on the moors. When I got older, of course, I joined in with the hunting and the drinking. Figgie never did though; he was an odd chap. Preferred eating pudding to hunting. He would never eat meat, even when he was a tiddler, but he could eat pudding all day."

There was one very important piece of information here; Ignatius Bowerman had a brother. There hadn't been a brother in any of the versions of 'Bowerman the Hunter' that I'd read on the internet; I made a note-in-my-head about this, then I decided that finding out more about Ignatius Bowerman's brother might give me more clues for my investigation.

So I asked, "Was Figgie short for something? It's quite a strange name."

"His real name was Daniel, but he used to eat so much pudding that the cook called him 'Figgie'. When Father heard the name, he thought that it was very funny; so funny that he stopped calling Daniel by his real name and called him 'Figgie' all of the time."

"Did Daniel mind being called 'Figgie'?"

I asked this question because I hate it if anyone calls me Tom. They're wrong if they do, because my name is Thomas. I don't shorten anybody's name out loud and I won't answer if they shorten mine.

(Just occasionally I shorten Scarlett Jones' name to 'Scar' in my head, because she is so evil and nasty).

"He didn't mind being called 'Figgie' when we were boys, but I think he probably minded more as we got older. He knew Father preferred me because I loved hunting and drinking. Figgie liked books and poetry. I was the eldest, the strongest and the fittest. Figgie was shorter and all the puddings he ate made him rotund."

I wasn't quite sure what 'rotund' meant, but it sounded like a word that might mean fat, and sometimes people do get fat if they eat too much food.

"What happened to Daniel?"

"Who's Daniel?" Ignatius Bowerman had obviously forgotten what our conversation had been about. I tried again.

"Figgie, Daniel, your brother. What happened to him?"

"Ah! Figgie was the first to know I hadn't come home that night. We shared a bedroom you see. He knew that I'd gone out to chase a hare without telling Father, and didn't want me to get a beating; so he went looking for me. I think the witches must have found him, because now he's a rock too."

This was really significant information for my investigation. It was significant because;

1. It meant that there was another talking rock on Dartmoor.
2. Daniel *(Figgie)* might know where his brother's hounds were.

I was so excited, my voice sounded a bit squeaky when it came out of my throat. I asked three questions, one after the other.

"How do you know he is a rock too? Where is he? Do you go and see him?"

"That is a lot of questions to ask a tired old rock, who has been hunting for his hounds all night. Which one would you like me to answer first?"

"Sorry Mr Bowerman." I wasn't sorry but I knew, *(because Mum explained it to me once)* that you sometimes have to say 'sorry' even when you don't think you have done anything wrong. Apparently it makes people feel less grumpy. *(I don't understand why)*. "I'll ask those questions one at a time. How do you know that Figgie is a rock now?"

"That's a silly question, boy. I know that Figgie is a rock because I sometimes go to visit him."

I didn't think that my question was at all 'silly', but I liked the rest of Ignatius Bowerman's answer because it answered another question as well. It answered the question, 'Do you go and see him?'

"Where is Daniel? Is he on Dartmoor?"

"Who is Daniel?" Ignatius Bowerman had obviously forgotten what we were talking about again.

When I replied, my voice sounded a bit louder and a bit crosser than it had before. "Where is your brother Daniel? Your brother Daniel who is also called Figgie, and who is also a rock; where is he now?"

"Oh, I see. Why didn't you say that before? Figgie lives on the other hill. I sometimes go to visit him. You should come with me, I'd like to introduce you to him."

It was just around that time (11.32pm) that I started to feel two things:

1. I started to feel exasperated with Ignatius Bowerman.
2. I started to feel cold.

('Exasperated' is a word that means very, very annoyed. When you feel exasperated, you feel like giving up the thing that you're doing. I'm quite stubborn and I hardly ever give up, but I didn't want to ask very many more questions that night).

Being exasperated and cold is not any fun at all, and I wondered if Daniel Bowerman would be better at remembering, than his brother, Ignatius Bowerman.

So I said, "Mr Bowerman, I'd really like to visit your brother, and ask him some questions about your hounds. Can you tell me where he is?"

"I told you, he is on the other hill."

It was definitely time to go home.

"There are lots of hills round here. How am I supposed to know which hill Figgie is on?"

"I could take you there. I know the way."

I thought about what Ignatius Bowerman had said, there were two problems with his suggestion:

1. I wasn't sure that I could keep up with him.
2. I wasn't sure he'd remember how to find

his brother.

It was clear that Ignatius Bowerman sometimes remembered how to find things, and sometimes didn't. If I decided to go with him, I knew there was a risk that we would end up in the wrong place. I thought carefully about this risk for twenty seconds, and decided that it was a risk worth taking. Dad doesn't say very much when we visit him in prison, but before he went there, he used to say, 'Nothing ventured, nothing gained.' I think this means that you won't get a thing you want, if you don't do tricky things to try and get that thing. In my case, this meant I wouldn't get the information I needed about Ignatius Bowerman's hounds, if I didn't go with him to visit his brother.

It was too late to go anywhere that night (11.34pm), and despite my jacket, I was starting to shiver; so I decided I'd go back to my bedroom, and go with Ignatius Bowerman another night.

"I think that it would be a good idea for you to take me to visit Figgie sometime," I said to Ignatius Bowerman, "I could ask him some questions about your hounds."

"I'm very pleased to hear that," said Ignatius Bowerman in a pleased sounding voice, "Figgie didn't much like the hounds; they scared him, but he did like Rocky. Rocky loved Figgie almost as much as he loved me."

I shivered some more, and hoped I wasn't getting hypothermia. I know a lot about hypothermia, because I want to be a forensic scientist. For example, I knew that if my body temperature dropped below 35°C on Hayne Down, there was a chance I might get confused. I didn't want to be confused, so I decided to get home quickly.

I said, "Okay then, next time I come to visit you, we'll go and see if we can find Figgie." By then I'd given up trying to use Daniel's real name. "But now I'm cold and I must go home."

"I'm always cold," replied Ignatius Bowerman, "unless the sun's shining on me, then I warm up."

I didn't want to tell him then that he couldn't be 'always cold', if he was warmed by the sun some of the time. I didn't want to tell him, because I wanted to go back to my bedroom and warm myself up. I stood up, and it was then that I remembered my two problems:

1. I'd dropped my torch.
2. It was too dark to see my way down to my house.

I was worried about both of these problems. I was worried, because I knew that not being able to see meant that I'd have to stay where I was until it got light. This made me even more worried, because I knew that if I stayed where I was until it got light, I'd definitely get hypothermia and be confused. I thought for sixteen seconds about this problem and decided that I definitely needed to do something. The problem was, I didn't know what the 'something' was that I needed to do.

Usually, in these sorts of situations, it's the right thing to ask someone for help. I could have asked my Mum for help if I'd been at home, or I could have asked Mrs Aitken for help if I'd been at school. But I wasn't in either of those places. I was on Dartmoor, at night, in my pyjamas.

What I needed was a way of seeing in the dark. It was a big problem that required even more thinking time; so I decided to think about it for another twenty seconds. It was after seventeen and a half seconds, I thought these very useful thoughts;

1. Ignatius Bowerman sometimes went looking for his hounds at night.
2. Even moving-slash-talking rocks can't look for things without seeing.
3. Ignatius Bowerman must be able to see in the dark.

Maybe, Ignatius Bowerman could help me to find my way home.

So I said, "Excuse me, Mr Bowerman, please can I ask you a favour?"

"Oh hello Thomas, I didn't see you there," he replied, "of course you can. I'm at your service."

I hoped that the fact that Ignatius Bowerman had said that he 'didn't see me' was because he'd forgotten that I was there again, and not because he couldn't see in the dark.

I asked another question, "I need to go home

now, because I'm cold, and I can't see in the dark. Please can you help me to find my way?"

"It would be my pleasure, where do you live?"

"I live in the house across the lane. You might not remember it because you're not very good at remembering places; but please could you look and see if you can see it?"

There was the same creaking noise that I'd heard when Ignatius Bowerman had sat down, and I estimated that it was him standing up. I took a step back because I didn't want him to forget that I was there, and tread on me. Being trodden on by a rock, even a forgetful, talking one, was not an idea that I liked.

Ignatius Bowerman said, "I can see a lane and a small house."

"That's my house!" I didn't think it was a particularly 'small' house because it had four bedrooms, a bathroom, a kitchen, a dining room *(that we didn't use)* and a big lounge; but I thought that maybe Ignatius Bowerman's father's house had been quite big, because he'd said that they had lots of parties. "Please can you show me how to get there?"

"I can do better than that young Thomas. I can take you there."

This time, I only had one second to think about what Ignatius Bowerman had said because, before I knew what was happening, he'd picked me up round the waist and put me under one of his arms.

It seems unlikely that you, person who is reading my non-story, have ever been held, high up in the air, under a moving-slash-talking rock's armpit. But you can do imagining, and can probably imagine what it felt like when I tell you that a rock armpit is not like a human armpit. Human armpits are warm, damp and soft; rock armpits are cold, hard and sharp. I was held tightly in a cold, hard and sharp place. When Ignatius Bowerman started to move, the rock armpit banged against my body in a very uncomfortable way. It felt as though my ribs were going to break; but the worst thing was, that he'd picked me up so I was looking straight up at the sky. Two things were bad about this:

1. My cap fell off.
2. I couldn't see where we were going.

It didn't seem like the right time for politeness, so I said, "Ow! Put me down immediately! You're hurting me!"

"But I thought you said that you wanted to go home?" Ignatius Bowerman sounded confused, but he didn't stop walking.

"I do want to go home, but I don't want to get there with broken ribs." I tried tugging at the rock arm that held me but it wouldn't budge.

"I broke my ribs once, and my finger. I did it falling off a horse. I went back out hunting that weekend." Ignatius Bowerman continued striding down the hill.

"Well I don't want to break my ribs, my finger or any part of me!" I was very cross now and probably sounded it.

I wriggled around, but there was no way that I was going to get out of Ignatius Bowerman's vice-like grip.

(Mrs Aitken told me that being in a 'vice-like grip' is a good way of saying you're held so tight that

you can't move).

"We're nearly at your house. Please stop wriggling," Ignatius Bowerman replied.

Wriggling was hurting me, so I stopped. Ignatius Bowerman's enormous strides were moving us so efficiently; that I knew it wouldn't take much longer for me to get home. I gave up arguing and leant my head back as far as it would go, to try and see where we were. It was still dark, so all I could actually see was a square light. This confused me, the light came from where I thought my bedroom window should be, and I knew I'd turned my bedroom light off, before I'd crept out earlier that night. I put my head back up straight; because my neck was hurting, and thought of two reasons that my light might be on:

1. I'd forgotten to turn it off.
2. Mum had turned it on.

I knew that I hadn't forgotten to turn the light off, because turning it off had been part of my plan, and I never forget things that are in my plans. This meant Mum must have turned the light on, and very importantly, this meant that Mum knew I wasn't in my bed. I leant my head back again, to check that the light had been shining from my bedroom window, and not from Mum's. Checking proved impossible; not because I was upside down, but because, when I leant my head back again, there were no lights on at all.

By then, I could tell by the crunch of gravel underneath his feet *(if they were feet)*, that Ignatius Bowerman was carrying me up the drive. This worried me because there was a chance that Mum was awake, and I really didn't want her to hear me being carried up the drive in the armpit of a rock. I decided to see whether being really polite to Ignatius Bowerman would make him put me down.

(Mum says that even if being polite is tricky, it is a good way to get people to do what you want them to do).

I cleared my throat in a polite kind of way, and said in a very clear voice. "Excuse me Mr Bowerman, your Lordship."

120

It was then that I heard Ignatius Bowerman laughing for the first time. You would probably imagine *(because you can do imagining)* that a rock's laugh would sound completely different to a person's laugh; but you would have been wrong. A rock's laugh sounds exactly like a person's laugh and furthermore *(another long word that is two short words joined together)*, when a rock laughs, his belly shakes just like a person's belly.

"Ho, ho, ho! Your Lordship! That's the best joke I've heard for three hundred years."

I wondered then whether Ignatius Bowerman had heard any other jokes at all in the last three hundred years, but I didn't ask him about that. I had more important things to say.

For example, I particularly needed to say, "Shhh! Please be quiet, Mr Bowerman. My Mum might hear you."

Ignatius Bowerman stopped laughing and stood still.

"You have a mother?"

This seemed like an odd thing for a rock-slash-person to ask, until I remembered that

Ignatius Bowerman's mother had died when he was young. It made me sad for him; mothers can be annoying, but they're very important.

So I used a gentle voice, "Yes, I do have a mother. I'll tell you about her one day, but today we need to be very quiet so she can't hear us and stop me from coming to see you."

"I can be very quiet," said Ignatius Bowerman, in a medium-to-loud voice, "Do you want to get down now?'

"Yes, please," I whispered, hoping that he'd copy me and whisper as well.

Before I knew it *(this is a silly phrase but Mrs Aitken says it means 'very quickly')* Ignatius Bowerman had let go of my legs, and was dangling me by my armpits, about a metre above the ground. I didn't like being dangled.

"Can you jump from here?" he asked *(not very quietly)*.

"I think so," I whispered; I didn't really think so, but I didn't want us to make any more noise than we needed to, "can you lower me a little bit more?"

And again before I knew it, Ignatius Bowerman

had lowered me down to the ground in front of him, and let go of my armpits. It was nice to be standing back on the ground and not dangling from a rock-slash-person.

I turned round to face Ignatius Bowerman, and had a strange urge to hug him *(or at least his leg, which was the only part of him that I could reach)*. This urge was strange because:

1. People sometimes hug trees, but they don't usually hug rocks.
2. I don't really do hugging.

In the end, I didn't hug Ignatius Bowerman that day, I don't really know why. *(You'll see, if you carry on reading my non-story, that I did hug him another day)*.

Instead, I patted him on the knee and said, "Thank you very much, Mr Bowerman. I can find my way into the house now. Can you find your way back onto Hayne Down?"

I half expected Ignatius Bowerman to ask me where Hayne Down was then; but he didn't. He patted me on the head *(luckily his pat was gentle and didn't knock me out)*, and turned round to stride back up the drive.

"Goodbye young Thomas. I look forward to your next visit."

I only saw him take two strides, because his strides were so long and also it was still dark. I shivered and remembered I was very cold, so I turned round and walked back to the house. I was so tired I didn't notice some things that I really should have noticed. I didn't notice that:

1. I could see where I was going.
2. The porch light was on.
3. Mum was standing in the porch.

Six
A Dartmoor Map

I thought for ten seconds about what to do next. I didn't think Mum would have seen Ignatius Bowerman, because it was dark, but she might have heard him. This was good and bad:

1. It was good, because she would have thought he was a man, and not a rock.
2. It was bad, because mums don't like their sons talking to strange men on the drive at night.

I didn't think Mum had seen me either, but I couldn't be sure. It seemed likely she knew that I wasn't asleep in my bed. I thought of three things that I could do. They were:

1. Turn around, and go back up the drive.
2. Try to sneak round to the back door, and get back in my bed.
3. Go to the front door and say, 'hello' to Mum.

I knew that I couldn't do number one, because I was already shivering and didn't want to get hypothermia and get confused. I knew that I could probably do number two, but I didn't know if the back door would be locked. That meant that my only option left was number three, and I didn't want to do that one either.

Just then I realised that I wasn't going to have to choose any of the options. I realised it because I couldn't see, and I realised that I couldn't see because Mum was shining a torch in my face.

"Thomas, what are you doing?" Mum called.

I didn't think I could pretend to be anybody else, because when someone shines a torch on your face, they can usually see who you are.

"Hello Mum," I answered, because it was all that I could think of to say. Normally, in this sort of situation, you would tell somebody what you had been doing. I couldn't do that, because I'd been talking to a moving-slash-talking, rock-slash-person. I started walking slowly towards the torchlight and said, "Please could you stop shining the torch in my eyes?" I said 'please', because I wanted Mum to not be cross with me, and being polite can stop people being cross with you. Mum pointed the torch at the ground in front of me, and watched me walk up the rest of the drive. At least, I presume that she watched me. I can't think of anything else that she might have been doing in the porch in the dark. I couldn't see what she was doing because:

1. It was dark.

2. I could see blue blobs in front of my eyes.

As I was walking towards the porch, I thought about some of the things Mum might say to me. I thought that she might be cross and say telling off things like, 'What on earth are you doing out here at night?' or 'Right, that's it, you're grounded.'

('Grounded' is a punishment that means that you're not allowed to go out with your friends. It's

not a very good punishment for me, because I don't have any friends, and I quite like being inside).

I also thought that Mum might have said worried things like, 'Have you any idea how dangerous this is?' or 'Why are you wearing your pyjamas outside?' But when I got to the porch, Mum didn't look worried or cross, and she didn't say any of those things.

What she did say was, "You must be freezing. Go up to bed, and I'll bring you some hot chocolate."

She said this at the same time as giving me a hug, and I couldn't see whether or not she was winking at me. *(I've told you before that Mum winks when she is teasing me).* So I did the only sensible things that I could think of; I took my jacket and trainers off, went into the house, went up the stairs, went into my bedroom and got into my bed. Then I got out of bed again, because I remembered that my striped pyjama bottoms were wet from the puddle; I took these off, put my red pyjamas bottoms on and got back into bed. Then I got out of bed again, because I remembered that I didn't like wearing pyjama tops and bottoms that don't match; I took my striped top off, put my red top on, and got back into bed. By the time that I'd done all of that, I was feeling much warmer, but it was still nice to see the steam coming out of the mug of hot chocolate, that Mum brought into the room seven minutes later.

Mum gave me the hot chocolate mug and said, "Careful, it's hot." Mums say obvious things sometimes. *(Well, I don't know about your mum because I don't know her, but my Mum says obvious things. For example, she once said I was her favourite son. That was obvious, because I'm her only son).*

I took the mug carefully, "I know it's hot because it has steam coming out of it, but thanks for the warning."

Mum sat down on the end of my bed, and smiled, "Did you have a nice time out there tonight?"

I was so surprised at her question *(because I still expected her to be cross with me)*, that the only thing that I could think of to say was a very short thing.

I said, "Yes."

Mum didn't seem to mind my short answer, "I thought I heard talking; were you talking to someone in the drive?"

This was a very tricky question to answer. I didn't want to tell Mum that I'd been talking to a moving-slash-talking rock, and I didn't want to tell her a lie, because she thinks I always tell the truth. I had to think of an answer that wouldn't be a lie, and wouldn't make Mum worry.

So I said, "I wasn't talking to a person." Which was very, very nearly true because although Ignatius Bowerman had been a person before, he was a rock now.

If I was a mum *(which I'm clearly never going to be, because I'm a boy)*, I'd be a bit worried that my son had been outside, in the drive, at night, talking to something that wasn't a person. I'm not sure what I'd say or do, but I don't think that it would be what my mum said and did.

She said, "Next time you go out at night, wear

some warm clothes instead of your pyjamas. Goodnight, Thomas. Sleep well," and then she gave me a kiss on my head.

After that, Mum switched my bedside light on, turned the big light off, went out and closed the bedroom door. My bedroom looked fuzzy in the yellow light, and I started to feel very cosy under my duvet. As I sipped my hot chocolate, I thought about Ignatius Bowerman, his brother Daniel, who was also called Figgie, and my Mum. I was too tired to think about my investigation, and I fell asleep with my empty mug in my hand and my bedside light still on. I don't know what time it was.

The next day was Sunday, and I woke up at 9.48am with the mug still in my hand *(it had dribbled a little bit of chocolate onto my duvet cover)*. This was quite a late wake-up time for me, and I knew that Mum would be on her way to church. *(I don't believe in God so I don't go to church; except at Christmas, when not going to church is a bit like not going to someone's birthday party)*. The sun was shining in through my bedroom window, because the curtains were open. This was not what I was expecting, because I'd shut them before I crept outside to see Ignatius Bowerman. I estimated *(I don't like guessing)*, that Mum must have opened them, which meant that last night she'd been looking out of my bedroom window before I saw her shining her torch in the porch. I got out of bed quickly and went over to the window to see if I could see Ignatius Bowerman. He was there on Hayne Down, in his usual place, standing very still. I was relieved for two reasons to see that he was there:

1. It meant that I'd know where to find him when I crept out of my bed that night.
2. It was Sunday, and people often came to look at him on Sunday afternoons.

I thought about my mum, and the things that she'd said to me the night before. I wondered why she hadn't been really cross with me for being outside, when I should have been in bed. I thought about these things for thirty-two seconds; but couldn't think of any good answers to my questions. So I decided to think about my investigation instead; I knew that I wanted to meet Figgie-slash-Daniel, and ask him some questions about Ignatius Bowerman's hounds. To do this, I'd need to creep out of my bedroom again *(although Mum didn't seem to mind me going)* and wear some warmer clothes *(which Mum had told me to do)*. I'd also need to find a different torch to take with me. I knew I had lots of warmer clothes in my bedroom, but I didn't have a different torch. I decided I'd be more likely to find a different torch downstairs. Before going downstairs, I went to have a shower.

This didn't take me long, because I don't like having a shower. I quite like having a bath, because in the bath, you get lots of time to lie and think; but when you have a shower, you're busy getting all wet, and then you're busy getting all dry; and you can't really think while you're doing it. Once I was dressed, I went downstairs for my breakfast. On Sundays, I have to make my own breakfast. I always have four pieces of toast, *(because our toaster has four holes)*, with butter and Marmite on them, and a cup of orange juice. Scarlett Jones *(who is not a friendly girl)* once said to me that I smelt of Marmite. She was probably right, but I can't see how that could be a bad thing, because Marmite smells nice.

While I was eating my four pieces of Marmite and butter on toast, I thought about the things that I needed to do that day. I needed to:

1. Hoover my bedroom and the landing. *(That is one of my weekend chores).*
2. Sweep the path that goes all around the house. *(It's my job to keep it clear).*
3. Find out if Figgie-slash-Daniel was on the Dartmoor map. *(Part of my investigation).*
4. Find a different torch. *(So I could see where I was going later).*
5. Find out some information about Figgie-slash-Daniel on the internet.

I don't think that you, person who is reading my non-story, wants to hear about the time I spent hoovering, sweeping, talking to Granny on the phone, poking a package I found on the kitchen table, and drinking a cup of milk. You're probably much more interested in hearing about how I got on with my investigation into the whereabouts of Ignatius Bowerman's hounds.

I've already told you how much I like Google and how it works, so you'll understand now, when I tell you, that when I got back upstairs to my bedroom, I sat down at my desk, opened my laptop and typed the search term 'Daniel'. In 0.32 seconds, Google gave me 1,330,000,000 different pages to look at. If you're not very good at maths *(I'm very good at maths. For example, I know that 1,000,000,007 is the smallest prime number with ten digits)*, you might need me to tell you that 1,000,000,000 is one billion which is the same thing as one thousand million, except that we don't call it that. That is a lot of pages about the word, 'Daniel'; Google has a clever algorithm *(it is actually the computer programmers who are clever)* which decides which pages are the most important to your investigation, and puts them at the top of a list. This can save a lot of time, but it still took me a long time because I looked at thirty pages. On those thirty pages,

I found out nineteen fairly interesting things about the word 'Daniel', I'm only going to tell you three of them:

1. Daniel is another name that has a meaning. Daniel means, 'God is my judge'. *(I don't believe in God)*.
2. Daniel Craig who is an actor, who sometimes plays James Bond in films, supports Liverpool FC. *(I don't like football)*.
3. Daniel Goleman is a man who knows a lot about emotions. *(I don't really like emotions)*.

None of these fairly interesting things were any help at all with my investigation, so I knew that I needed to add another word to my search term. As Daniel's nickname was 'Figgie', I decided to type 'Daniel Figgie'; and Google gave me 20,700 results in 0.26 seconds. What was excellent about these results was that lots of them *(I looked at six)* gave the same information, and it was information that was going to be lots of help with my investigation. Here is the helpful information that I found;

1. Daniel-slash-Figgie was a tall rock on Dartmoor just like Ignatius Bowerman.
2. Daniel-slash-Figgie wasn't called Daniel or Figgie. He was called Figgie Daniel.
3. The internet didn't know that Figgie Daniel was Ignatius Bowerman's brother.
4. The internet didn't know that Figgie Daniel had once been a man.
5. The internet **did** know where Figgie Daniel was. He was on a hill called Easdon Hill.

Just as I was finding that helpful information, I heard the car drive up the drive. I waved to Mum out of my bedroom window, and went downstairs to see her. *(I wanted to carry on with my investigation, but it is friendly to go and say 'hello' to people when they come home).* Mum looked nice in her church clothes so I said, "Your skirt is the right length for God today. I hope he said he liked it." As I told Mum this, I winked at her, so that she'd know that I was teasing her, and not think that I'd started believing in God.

(Mrs Aitken taught me that the word 'God' has

to have a capital letter because, if you believe in him, he is very important).

"I think that was what he was saying," said Mum winking back, "but he might have been telling me I had the wrong colour lipstick on."

I was glad Mum had winked then, because I don't really understand lipstick, or anything that is make-up. The girls *(and the boys, but boys don't wear make-up)* aren't allowed to wear any at school; but sometimes they do. Scarlett Jones sometimes has so many pointy dark lines around her eyes; she looks like someone has punched her. *(Sometimes **I** feel like punching her)*. I really don't see the point of having rules, if people aren't going to obey them.

Mum always likes to have a cup of tea when she comes back from church, so I followed her into the kitchen, filled the kettle up and switched it on.

"You're a good lad," said Mum as she sat down at the table, "never any trouble, and you make a lovely cup of tea."

I knew Mum was exaggerating because I

sometimes do cause trouble, although not usually on purpose. For example, I caused trouble once by digging a hole on the beach, that was so big, a small boy fell into it and broke his nose. I argued at the time, that the small boy caused more trouble than me by actually doing the falling in; but the more I argued, the louder people's voices sounded, and the redder their faces got, so eventually, I stopped arguing.

I wanted to find out what was in the package that I'd been poking earlier; so when I sat down at the table opposite Mum, I pushed it around in front of me, to try and make her notice it. Mum didn't take any notice of my pushing around, so I asked her,

"What's in this package?"

"Hmm, I wonder if you can guess what it is," Mum replied, smiling.

I've already told you that I prefer estimating to guessing, so I tried to think of some clues that would help me to make a sensible estimate. It wasn't my birthday *(I've already told you my birthday is on August the 8th)*. It wasn't Mum's birthday, or Dad's birthday either, so it wasn't a birthday present. It wasn't Christmas, so it wasn't a Christmas present. I'd already decided that the package was cuboid shaped, so it could have been a book *(a cuboid has six faces and all of its faces are rectangles)*. I picked the package up *(I'd done this earlier as well as poking and looking at it)*, it wasn't very heavy, so it wasn't a big book.

I made my estimate, "I think it might be a book."

"It's not a book, but it is something that gives you information."

I thought about a question that I could ask.

"What sort of information?"

"Information about places about a specific place in fact. You'd better open it and see."

I was excited, I'd made another estimate about what might be inside the parcel, and I wanted to see if I was right. I pulled at the cardboard packaging, but it wouldn't open. Mum held out her hand.

"Let me see, ah yes, you have to open it this end. See, there's a label."

It wasn't like me to forget to read labels, but I think I did it this time because I was excited that the package might be what I'd estimated it would be. I slid my finger under the other end of the package, and it came open really easily. I peered inside. It was difficult to tell what was inside because it was in a plastic case, but I noticed two things;

1. It wasn't a book.
2. It was orange on the outside.

These two things meant that my estimate was almost certainly right. I looked at Mum.

"Is it a map?"

Mum nodded, "It's a map of Dartmoor. I thought we could both use it to go and find High Willhayes; but I thought that you might like to keep it in your bedroom, to help you with your research."

I looked carefully at Mum. She wasn't winking, so I understood she wasn't teasing me; but I wondered what she meant when she said 'research'. Could she possibly have guessed that I was doing an investigation? I pulled the map out of the packaging. It was orange and yellow and had a picture of a man standing on a tor on the front of it. The tor wasn't man-shaped enough to be Ignatius Bowerman, but it was still a tor.

"Thank you very much," I said to Mum, "it's exactly what I need for my research." I called it 'research' because I didn't want Mum to know that I was doing an investigation.

"I thought it might be," replied Mum, "it is exactly what I needed, when I was a girl and lived here in this house."

"Did you like to do exploring on Dartmoor when you were a girl?"

"Oh yes, I used to roam around all over this part of the moors. Children were allowed much more freedom, then. I know my way around quite well."

I thought about what Mum had just said. If she knew her way around Dartmoor 'quite well', then she might be able to help me to work out where Figgie Daniel was. I decided that it was safe to ask her about Figgie Daniel, because he wasn't the main reason for my investigation.

"I've been looking for information about a rock called Figgie Daniel."

"Oh really, did you find anything useful?" Mum had a funny little smile on her face when she said this. I didn't really understand the smile, it could have meant:

1. I'm just a little bit happy that you like the map.
2. I think that the name 'Figgie Daniel' is a funny one.
3. I know that you have been talking to a moving-slash-talking rock.

I dismissed the last idea *(this means that I took no notice of it)* because although an ordinary person who can do imagining, might be able to make up a moving-slash-talking rock; she wouldn't be very likely to believe that such a thing could be real. I decided that ideas number one and number two could both be right.

"I found out that it's on Easdon Hill, but I don't know where that is."

"Well, I don't know where to find Figgie Daniel, but I do know where Easdon Hill is. It's on Dartmoor, and quite near here. If you open your new map out, I'll show you."

I took the map out of its plastic packet, and opened it carefully on the table. Mum moved the tea mugs to one side. I knew that maps always had north at the top of them, and south at the bottom, so I positioned it that way in front of me. Mum came and sat on the chair next to me, so we could both look at the map the same way up. Spread out on the table, it looked just like the map I'd found on the internet, except I could see a much bigger area of the moor. I stood up and looked at the top of it. You could see where normal countryside ended, and the moors began, because there were almost no roads *(orange and yellow lines)* on the moor, and because I could read the names of tors and hills. I ran my finger across the map and read a few out loud;

"Scarey Tor, Rowtor, West Mill Tor, Cosdon Hill, Oke Tor, Yes Tor, High Willhayes...," I stopped and looked at Mum, "Mum, I've found High Willhayes."

"Yes, you have," said Mum, "and we'll go

there one day. But if you're looking for Easdon Hill, you need to look much further south and east than you're now."

I sat down again and ran my finger to the right across the map and then down. I couldn't find Easdon Hill or Hayne Down.

"Dartmoor has a lot of hills," I said to Mum, "how am I supposed to know where to look?"

"It's easy to find things on maps when you know how," Mum said. "Most places have a number called a grid reference linked to them. Do you remember reading a six digit number for Figgie Daniel?"

"734822" I said, without hesitation. I hadn't realised that I'd remembered the number, but that happens to me a lot. "It had the letters SX in front of it."

"The SX tells us that the grid reference relates to this area. The whole of the UK is split up into a grid, and each area has a different two letter code."

"What's the code for London?"

Mum laughed, "I don't remember using this

sort of map in London; street maps are better in cities. You'll have to look it up. Do you want me to show you how to use the grid reference?"

I knew that if I went upstairs and looked at the internet, I'd probably be able to work out how to use the grid reference to find Figgie Daniel; but I also knew that Mum liked teaching me things.

So I said, "Yes, please. Is it to do with these blue numbers along the sides of the map?" I ran my finger down one side and along the bottom of the map, to show Mum what I meant.

"That's right," she said, "it's quite easy really. You just have to remember to read the along numbers first, and then the up numbers second. Where do you think 734822 might be?"

I looked at the blue numbers along the bottom of the map; they went from 50 to 80. The first two numbers of Figgie Daniel's grid reference were 73 so I estimated that he might be somewhere up the blue 73 line. I ran my finger slowly up the line. Just over the right of it, I could see Bowerman's Nose and Hayne Down, but they were nearer to the 74 line. I continued moving my finger upwards and there, with its capital E right on the 73 line, was Easdon Tor. I ran my finger around the square to the right of the 73 line, but couldn't see the words, Figgie Daniel. I found Easdon Hill, Easdon Down, Whooping Rock, Hut Circles and Cairn, but no Figgie Daniel. I looked at the grid reference again.

"Why are there six numbers when the blue lines only have two numbers each?"

"Good question." Mum answered, "The third number is to divide the square between the 73 line and the 74 line into ten sections. 734 means line 73 and four sections across. 822 means line 82 and two sections up. Where those two meet will be where your rock is."

I found the 82 line that went across the map, and put my finger where it met the 73 line. Then I estimated four tenths across and two tenths up. I tapped the map.

"Figgie Daniel must be just there, where the capital E for Easdon Hill is."

"Well done, but you need to understand that

a six figure grid reference gives you a hundred metre square of land. You would still have to look for Figgie Daniel even if you were in the right square."

I looked at the map again. It was going to be dark when I went there with Ignatius Bowerman, unless the moon was shining *(it doesn't actually shine)*, I wasn't going to be able to see 100 metres. There was a chance that Ignatius Bowerman was going to be able to find his brother without my help; but he was forgetful and I knew that I'd feel safer if I'd some idea of where I was going. I decided that I'd take the map with me.

That afternoon, I took more time preparing to creep out of the house than I'd done on my previous visits to Ignatius Bowerman. I laid out two fleeces, some thick jogging bottoms, some long socks, my red scarf, and the 'Devon' woolly hat that Granny had bought me when we moved here. *(I was a bit sad about losing my favourite baseball cap, but only a bit)*. I also found a torch. I found this torch in a place that I wasn't expecting to find it; I found it in the drawer that

I keep my fleeces in. I knew that I hadn't put it in that drawer myself, so it had to have been Mum who did it. I was pleased that she had, but a bit confused about her motives *(I've already told you what motives are)*. Mum really wasn't behaving like mums usually behave, but then I don't know everybody's mum. The torch was perfect for what I was going to do, because it had two batteries and was small enough to fit in the pocket at the front of my fleece. I put it on the bed with my warm clothes and decided *(again)* not to think too much about Mum's motives.

The other thing I put on the bed was the Dartmoor map *(Mum had said that I could keep it upstairs)*. I looked at the map on the bed and decided to do something with it. The map was folded up; this made it look neat and tidy, but it hid and all of the useful, where-things-are information. I opened it up like I had on the kitchen table and looked at it again; it would be very difficult to carry a map that was open like that. So I decided to fold it; I folded it so that I could still see Hayne Down and Easdon Hill, but so that it was small enough to fit in my fleece pocket with my torch. Now I don't know, person who is reading my non-story, if you've ever tried to keep a brand new map folded in the way that you want it to be. I've only done it once, but let me tell you, it's very difficult. Maps have their own fold lines that bounce open if you try to fold them to wrong way. I only took five seconds to think of a solution for this problem though; I opened my bedside table and took out one of the thirteen red elastic bands that were in there. *(Sometimes the postman drops the elastic bands that hold piles of letter together, I find them when I sweep round the house).* I used the elastic band to hold the map as I wanted it, and then I put it on my bed, next to the torch and my clothes.

For the rest of the afternoon and evening, I had some homework to do. I like to keep all of my homework until Sunday and do it all at once. Most ordinary people don't like homework, but I prefer it to being at school. I can usually find the answers out on the internet; and in my bedroom there isn't anybody making too much noise or throwing pencils. I did my maths homework first, because that's my favourite; it was algebra, which I'm very good at. Then I did my French homework *(French has a capital letter because it is a language)*. This was a silly homework because it was all about the names of different shops. I don't think people really go to butchers and greengrocers anymore, most people just go to Tesco's or Sainsbury's. Even though it was a silly homework, I was very good at it too. After chemistry *(no capital letter)* and food technology *(which is a long name for 'cooking')*, I only had my English *(capital letter)* homework to do.

I think you, person who is reading my non-story, should know by now, that although I like my English teacher Mrs Aitken very much, I find English quite difficult. Some English things are easy, like spellings and punctuation; they nearly always follow rules, and I like rules. The things in English that I find very difficult are the ones that need imagination. The English homework that I had to do was a 'Project Homework'. A 'Project Homework' is one that lasts for a whole half term, you're supposed to work on a bit of it each week. Usually I'm very good at 'Project Homeworks' because I get them done right at the beginning of the half term; but this English 'Project Homework' was due in in two weeks, and I hadn't even started it. There was a good reason for me not starting the homework, and that was because it was to write a story about the place where you live.

I really, really can't write stories. Mrs Aitken knows I find them difficult, but she was busy when I went to see her about it, and she just told me to do my best. I know that stories have a beginning, a middle and an end. In the beginning you're supposed to talk about the characters and the place where the characters are, in the middle, you explain the problem and at the end, you solve the problem. Because I can't do imagining, I can't do lots of the bits of writing a story. I can't describe characters and places that don't really exist, I can't invent problems, and if I haven't invented a problem, I can't invent a solution to it.

I looked at the homework instructions in my planner and thought about my story-writing project homework. The story had to be about the place where I lived. I lived in a house *(not very exciting)*, down a drive *(not very exciting)* near to Hayne Down *(a bit more exciting)*. Hayne Down was a bit more exciting, because it was where Ignatius Bowerman lived. It was as I was thinking this thought about Hayne Down that a really good idea came to me. I could write about Ignatius Bowerman and my investigation, and pretend that it was a story. I didn't know if writing about something that was real, still counted as a story, but I thought that most people would think that it was a story and not real. They would think this because:

1. Rocks don't usually move and talk.
2. Ignatius Bowerman was already a legend *(which is a type of story)*.
3. They would be able to do imagining.

So I started writing my non-story, and because you're reading it, you'll understand why I chose to call it a non-story. It is the only type of story that I know how to write, it might be the only story that I ever write; it doesn't need me to imagine, because it's all true. I've just now, right this second, decided that the best stories are the ones that are very true, but very nearly unbelievable. I really hope Mrs Aitken likes it.

Seven
Apologising to Trees

That night, Mum went to bed at half past eight, which was a lot earlier than usual. When she put her head around the door to say goodnight to me, she said all of the usual Sunday night things like, 'Have you packed your school bag?' 'Have you brushed your teeth?' and 'I love you.' And then she said something else.

She said, "Two jumpers are a lot warmer than one."

This seemed to me to be a strange thing for someone to say to someone who they think is going to bed; but you, person who is reading my non-story, might think that it was perfectly normal.

So I just said, "You're right Mum, two jumpers are warmer than one. Night night."

The good thing about Mum going to bed so early was that it meant that I could go and visit Ignatius Bowerman earlier than I had last time. This was a really good thing, because I wanted Ignatius to take me to visit his brother Figgie Daniel. Even though I could see on the Dartmoor map that Hayne Down and Easdon Hill were only two kilometres apart *(that is the same as one and a quarter miles)*; I thought that it would take quite a long time to get there with a moving-slash-talking-slash-forgetting rock.

I didn't want to waste any of my extra time, so as soon as Mum had shut my bedroom door, I put on the jogging bottoms, the long socks, the red scarf, the 'Devon' woolly hat and the two fleeces that I'd laid out on the bed. The map was still folded, so that Hayne Down and Easdon Hill were showing, and I put that and the torch into the pocket on the front of my top fleece. I was ready to creep out of the house again. This time though, I had an idea in my head that I didn't really need to creep; that maybe Mum knew that I was going out. I didn't really have time to think about this idea too much.

When I got to the porch, I thought that wellies or big boots would have been good things to put on for travelling across Dartmoor; but I didn't have either of those, so I just put my trainers on again. It wasn't quite as dark outside as it had been the last time I crept out of my house. The moon was shining *(you should know by now that the moon doesn't actually shine)* and even without the torch, I could see the fence and I could nearly see the end of the drive. I started walking up the middle of the drive, being careful to walk around the puddle that had got both my striped pyjama legs wet last time. As I got nearer to the end of the drive, I noticed something strange, I noticed that there was a big rock shape in the middle of the lane. I thought that this was strange because:

1. Lanes are for cars, and cars can't drive through rocks.
2. People don't usually build lanes, without moving big rocks out of the way first.

I estimated *(I don't like guessing)* that the rock was Ignatius Bowerman. I mainly estimated this because:

1. As I walked nearer, I realised that the rock was moving.
2. The only moving rock that I knew was Ignatius Bowerman. *(I didn't know whether or not Figgie Daniel could move).*

Although it was a good thing that I'd already found Ignatius Bowerman, there was also a bad thing happening; Ignatius Bowerman was walking away from the end of my drive and down the lane. Now, you people who are reading my non-story might think that a young man like me *(I was eleven, and I'm still eleven unless you are reading this non-story when I am another age)* should be able to catch up with an old rock *(he was at least but not exactly three hundred).* This would be true, except that the old rock was very tall and walked with very, very long steps. I was going to estimate then, how many of my steps would fit into one of Ignatius Bowerman's; but I didn't have time because I knew that I needed to catch him up.

I did something else instead of estimating. I did running!

Now I don't know about you, person who is reading my non-story, but I really don't like running. I don't like running because:

1. I'm not very good at it, and always come last in races.
2. If someone has to run for something *(like a bus)* it usually shows that they're not very organised.

I think that I was organised, *(I almost always am)* because I had the right clothes and equipment with me; but I still needed to run because I needed Ignatius Bowerman to show me where his brother was.

I ran as fast as I could, but by the time I got to the end of the drive, Ignatius Bowerman was striding *(strides are very big steps)* down the hill towards the bottom of the lane. Running was the only way that I could think of to catch up with him, so I kept on running. After about twenty five metres down the lane, I started to shout Ignatius Bowerman's name. I shouted it over and over again, but he didn't hear me. I knew that he didn't hear me because:

1. He didn't turn around.
2. He didn't shout my name back at me.

I kept running after Ignatius Bowerman. I was running so much that it was making me breathe with deep breaths, and I could see water vapour coming out of my mouth. My chest was starting to hurt, but I kept on running. *(I was breathing like that because when you run, your muscles use up oxygen and you need to breathe more of it in).*

I thought then, after I'd run for three minutes, that I'd probably have to stop running after a total of five minutes. It was after four minutes and twelve seconds, that I noticed some important things about Ignatius Bowerman:

1. He was still in front of me.

2. He was still moving, but he wasn't moving away from me.
3. He wasn't moving by walking, he was moving by wriggling and waving his rock-arms around.

Although my chest was hurting so much now that I really wanted to stop running, I didn't stop; I knew that it was important for me to catch Ignatius Bowerman up, because I needed to visit Figgie Daniel before I could carry on with my investigation.

I tried shouting again. "Oi! Ignatius Bowerman!" But he didn't turn round and see me. Next, I shouted, "It's Thomas!" *(This was a sensible thing to shout because he wasn't looking at me and couldn't see me).* Unfortunately, Ignatius Bowerman just kept on waving his rock-arms around and wriggling. Because I was still running, and because Ignatius Bowerman wasn't moving away from me, I was starting to catch up with him. I stopped running and tried one more, much longer shout. I wanted it to be the loudest shout that I could do, so I waited six breaths until I was breathing more normally. **"King, Lustleigh, Grim, Bovey, Raven, Hunter, Rocky!"** These were, of course, the names of Ignatius Bowerman's missing hounds. I thought that hearing his hounds' names might make Ignatius Bowerman hear me; and I was right! As I stood at the highest point in the lane, looking down on Ignatius Bowerman; he stopped wriggling and waving his rock-arms around, and turned his rock-body around to see who had shouted.

"Thomas, there you are, my boy! Where have you been? I've been searching for you everywhere."

I thought that this probably wasn't true because:

1. Ignatius Bowerman could usually only remember about his hounds, and had probably forgotten about me.
2. Nobody has actually been 'everywhere'.

I decided that it didn't really matter if Ignatius Bowerman had been searching for me or not. What mattered was that he'd seen me, and that he'd remembered my name. I started to jog down the lane *(jogging is slow running)*, and as I got closer, I could see why he'd been waving his rock-arms around and wriggling. Ignatius Bowerman was all tangled up with the trees at the bottom of the lane. These trees weren't like usual trees at the side of a road, they didn't have straight trunks that pointed up towards the sky; these trees were bent and curly, and they had bent and curled into a tunnel-shape over the road. This tunnel shape would have been big enough for a horse or car to go through, but it wasn't big enough for a moving-slash-talking rock. *(It wasn't big enough for a bus either, which is why I have to walk to a car park to catch my school bus)*. If I could do imagining, I'd tell you that it looked as though the trees had fingers that were grabbing on to Ignatius Bowerman, and holding him back; but I can't do imagining and I think that the branches *(that did look a bit like fingers)* were probably just touching him, because he was a very tall rock-slash-person, and much too wide for the lane.

As I got closer to Ignatius Bowerman, I thought I could see a solution to his problem. *(It was my problem as well because I needed his help to find Figgie Daniel).*

I shouted, "Stand still, Mr Bowerman! Don't move until I get there."

Ignatius Bowerman shouted back, "I'm in a bit of a predicament; these darned trees won't let go of me. I'm finding it most frustrating because I need to go and look for my hounds."

I'd never heard a rock shout before. I wasn't surprised to find out that it sounded just like a rock speaking, but a lot louder. I could see that Ignatius Bowerman was still wriggling, but he wasn't waving his rock-arms around any more. I thought that this was because his rock-arms had got so tangled up in the trees that he couldn't move them.

I was getting very close to the tangled-slash-moving-slash-talking rock; but I still needed to shout, "Stand still and I'll come to help you. I'm going to help you to find your hounds with my investigation."

Ignatius Bowerman didn't do what I suggested and stay still; he wriggled even more and tried to turn his whole body around so that he was facing me properly. I was worried that he would get even more tangled up in the trees if he didn't stop wriggling, so I started jogging down the hill towards him again.

When I got there, I could see that the tangled-slash-moving-slash-talking rock problem was even more of a problem than I'd first thought it was. Ignatius Bowerman was so tangled up in the branches it looked as though the branches were moving closer around him. Some of the trees' roots were even wrapped around his ankles.

"Please could you stop wriggling, Mr Bowerman, so that I can see how to help you," I said.

"I'll try," replied Ignatius Bowerman, "but I'm not going to find it easy. These trees are a nuisance; they always do this to me."

And with that, he stopped wriggling quite so much. His arms were still moving backwards and forwards a bit, and pulling against the tree branches, but the rest of his body was still.

I was interested in what Ignatius Bowerman had said to me. I thought that he'd tangled himself in the trees, but he obviously thought that the trees were causing the problem on purpose.

"Are you sure that the trees are doing it? It looks as though you've got tangled because you're too tall and wide for this bit of the lane."

"Oh yes! I definitely know that the trees are doing it. Trees are very mischievous; they like growing in places, and doing things that annoy other people. They're like **naughty children**, that is why people sometimes **chop them down**." Instead of saying, 'naughty children' and 'chop them down' in his normal voice, Ignatius Bowerman turned back towards the trees and shouted the words at them. I think that there must have been some wind then, because the branches that weren't holding on to Ignatius Bowerman waved around a bit.

When I reached Ignatius Bowerman, I looked at him carefully and thought about what he'd said about trees being mischievous *(that means naughty)*. The branches did look as though they were holding onto him; they were wrapped around his rock-arms and were leaning in towards them. I wondered if trees could really be 'mischievous'. It didn't seem possible to a boy who can't do imagining; but if rocks could move and talk then maybe trees could do naughty things. I could think of two possible times that I'd heard about trees being 'mischievous':

1. One time, when we'd lived in London and my father wasn't busy stealing money he'd explained that the bumps in our road were because of the tree roots pushing up against the tarmac.

2. Sometimes in the autumn, the train from Plymouth to Exeter is very late because the trees have dropped their leaves all over the tracks. *(You can't get a train from anywhere near my house, so I don't go on one; but I do look at train delays on the internet).*

I couldn't decide whether the trees or Ignatius Bowerman himself had caused his problem; but my thinking had helped me to see that there was a solution that would work, whatever the cause had been.

So I said, "Mr Bowerman, I want you to listen very carefully. I'm going to give you two instructions, and you need to do both of them at once." I wasn't sure that giving him two instructions at once was a very good idea; because he wasn't very good at remembering even one thing at a time. "I want you to turn around carefully to face me and then walk slowly out of the trees towards me. At the same time, I want you to apologise to the trees for disturbing them."

"They should be apologising to me!" said Ignatius Bowerman very grumpily; "I didn't ask them to tangle me up."

I tried to be patient, "No you didn't, but you did walk down their lane and you're a lot bigger than them." *(Being patient is difficult for me because it involves imaging what other people (or rocks or trees) are feeling).*

"This is a very difficult situation for me,"

grumbled Ignatius Bowerman. "I'm a proud man and proud men should not have to apologise to silly trees who can't behave themselves." At this, the trees made a creaking noise and looked as though they might have been wrapping themselves around Ignatius Bowerman even more tightly than before. I tried hard to stay patient, but I didn't do it very well. I was cross with the trees, and with Ignatius Bowerman.

"Mr Bowerman, you're **not** a man! You're a rock! Stop being so proud, and help me to sort this situation out. I'm here because I want to help you to find your hounds, so please be sensible! You've annoyed the trees, and now you need to apologise to them." I didn't know if this was true about trees or not; but I do know, *(because my mum has told me)* that if you have annoyed somebody, a good way to stop them from being annoyed with you is to apologise. I've found out that apologising to annoyed people even works if you don't actually think that you have done anything wrong. Although this is a type of lying, I think it works because annoyed people are usually too busy shouting to do any proper thinking about whether you're really sorry or not.

What I'd said to Ignatius Bowerman about apologising must have worked, because just then, he turned himself slowly around so that his whole body was facing me. I stepped to the side of the lane onto the grass just in case he moved towards me quickly and stepped on me.

I said, "Well done! Now all you need to do is apologise and walk forwards very slowly." Ignatius Bowerman started to move, but it was clear that he was still too tangled in the trees to go more than one step. "Apologise!" I said, "Apologise to the trees!"

"I do not know how to apologise, Thomas," said Ignatius Bowerman, as he pulled against the tree branches. "I was a very proud man, and I was a very rich man. Proud, rich men do not have to apologise, so I haven't done it before."

That made sense to me, so I replied, "It isn't too difficult. You just have to say 'I'm sorry ... and then say the thing that you're sorry about."

"But I'm not sorry about anything." said Ignatius Bowerman, "I'm not sorry because I've not done anything to be sorry about."

"Apologies don't always work like that." I explained. "You can say sorry even if you're not really sorry. If the trees believe you, then they will probably let you go."

"Well, I hope you don't mind me saying; but that sounds like a very silly thing to me."

I stopped trying to be patient and shouted. "You think that's silly? You think apologising when you have disturbed something, is silly? You try being a boy in the night, talking to a rock about some hounds that he lost three hundred years ago, and telling him to apologise to trees! That is silly! Very silly indeed, and I'm not sure that I want to do it anymore!"

Ignatius Bowerman hung his rock-head. "I'm sorry Thomas," he said, "Please accept my humblest apologies, and please don't shout at me. I know that you're trying to help."

I looked carefully at the tall, tangled rock. I needed to look at him carefully to help me to decide whether he was pretend apologising or real apologising. His rock-eyes were looking at the ground and he'd reached out one of his rock-hands towards me. I decided that he was probably being sincere.

(*'Being sincere' is when you really mean what you say; the opposite to 'sincere' is 'sarcastic', which is when you don't really mean what, you say, and are trying to be a bit nasty. These things can get a bit confusing*).

"I accept your apology," I replied. "But as I said before, it is the trees that you need to apologise to, not me."

"I know," said Ignatius Bowerman in a quiet voice. He raised his head a little and looked back over his shoulder. "I'm very sorry, trees. Please accept my humble apologies, and please let me go. I promise that I won't come down your lane again."

I thought that this last bit was probably untrue, and that he was likely to forget within a day that the trees were even there; but his apology appeared to work. I had to look carefully, but I could see the trees start to release their grip on Ignatius Bowerman.

"Move forwards gently," I said, "take small steps, so that they don't panic." I'd no idea whether or not the trees were likely to panic, but small steps seemed like a good idea.

"It's working!" whispered Ignatius Bowerman. *(That was the first time that I'd heard a rock whisper)*. "They're letting me go."

"Keep moving forwards then. Nice and steady." I could see that he was right. As he moved forwards, the branches uncurled from around him and then sprang back into their 'tree-by-the-road' positions. Either the apology or the moving forward slowly was working; I wasn't sure which it was, but decided that, as long as Ignatius Bowerman got free, it didn't really matter how he'd done it.

Within one minute, Ignatius Bowerman was completely free from the trees and standing in the lane looking at me.

"Thank you, Thomas, you're a very clever boy. You're very good at understanding situations;

I must remember to listen to you more often." This was a nice thing for Ignatius Bowerman to say to me, but I knew that he wouldn't remember to listen to me more often, because he didn't remember anything very well. Although I was still curious about whether or not the trees had been holding on to Ignatius Bowerman on purpose, I decided that we'd wasted enough 'hound-finding' time that night already.

So I replied, "You're welcome. Please try to avoid trees in future. Can you take me to meet your brother now?"

"Do I have a brother?"

I sighed, this was going to be a long night. *('Going to be a long night' is a bit of a silly phrase as clearly the length of a night is decided by the time of year; not by the annoyingness of a walking-slash-moving-slash-forgetting rock).*

"You do have a brother, you told me about him. His name is Daniel but some people call him 'Figgie'."

"Oh, Figgie! Of course, why didn't you say that before? I'd love to take you to see Figgie.

Climb onto my shoulder." And with that, Ignatius Bowerman knelt down on the tarmac of the lane, and waited for me to do what he'd said.

Ignatius had forgotten something important again *(the thing was that he had a brother)*; but I didn't want to tell him. I didn't want to tell him because:

1. I thought that asking Figgie Daniel some questions would help me with my investigation.
2. Travelling on the shoulder of a moving-slash-talking rock was a very exciting idea.
3. We'd already wasted twenty-six minutes of the night, on untangling Ignatius Bowerman from the trees.

So I put my left foot onto his rock-knee and reached my right hand up his chest. I like climbing and Ignatius Bowerman had plenty of handholds and footholds, so it wasn't too difficult to climb up across his chest, onto his left shoulder. I sat down and decided that sitting on a rock-shoulder felt more comfortable than being held in a rock armpit, but it didn't feel very safe.

"I'm on your shoulder, but don't move yet," I told Ignatius Bowerman.

"I know that you're on my shoulder, because I can feel you there," the rock replied, "you're not very heavy are you?"

I didn't know how much I weighed, so I didn't answer that question. Instead I said. "Don't move yet, I'm making myself a seatbelt." I said this, because I'd decided that I might fall off Ignatius Bowerman's shoulder if I had to let go of him, to look at my map or shine my torch. I undid my red scarf from around my neck and put it around Ignatius Bowerman's neck instead. Next, I crossed over the ends of the scarf and tied them around my waist with a reef knot. *(I knew that the knot I tied was a reef knot because a video on the internet showed me how to do it).*

"Can I move now?" asked Ignatius Bowerman. "I'd like to go and see my brother Figgie. Have you met him?"

I was too excited to be grumpy about poor remembering skills. Sitting on the shoulder of a moving-slash-talking rock was a very exciting experience, even for a teenager who doesn't really get excited.

"Yes, we can go now," I replied, "let's go and find Figgie."

Eight
Finding Figgie

Things felt even more exciting when Ignatius Bowerman stood up; I was so high that I'd have had to reach down to touch the top of the trees. I didn't want to touch the top of the trees, I didn't want to go anywhere near the trees; I'd had enough of trees for one evening and suspected that Ignatius Bowerman felt the same.

"Which way do we need to go to find your brother?" I asked.

Ignatius Bowerman winced. *(That is, I think he winced, it's difficult to tell if a rock is wincing or not).* "I say!" He said, "There's no need to shout at me!"

I looked at him and realised that I was sitting right next to where his ear would have been *(if he was a man).* I spoke in a quieter voice, "I'm not shouting, but I'm sitting right next to your ear. Does that sound any better?"

"Yes, thank you, young Thomas. That's much better; I can hear you quite clearly. Now, what did you ask me?"

"I asked you which way we needed to go to find your brother Daniel."

"Shall we call him Figgie? That is his nickname; I'll tell you how he got it sometime. He lives on Easdon Hill, which is northwest of here, across some fields; but why do you want to meet him? He can be very annoying, you know. He is not sensible like me."

Ignatius Bowerman had obviously forgotten that he'd already told me how his brother Figgie had got his nickname. I wondered if I'd find Figgie as annoying as Ignatius obviously did, I don't like being annoyed. I haven't got a brother;

but if I did have, and my brother was me, I think that I'd really annoy myself.

I explained my reasons. "I want to meet him because I think that he might have some useful information about the whereabouts of your hounds."

"Oh, I see," said Ignatius Bowerman, "Figgie didn't like hounds, he was scared of them. They didn't like him either and used to snap at him when he walked past them."

"I'm not surprised he was scared of them if they snapped at him," I said, "but even if he didn't like them, he might have seen or heard something in the last three hundred years, that might help me to find them for you."

"It would be a wonderful thing if you found my hounds for me, Thomas. I miss them very much. I miss my brother too despite him being annoying, but please do not tell him that I said so."

My first journey on the shoulder of a walking-slash-talking rock was an interesting one. It was interesting because:

1. I had never had a journey like that before.
2. I could see lots of things because the moon was bright and Ignatius Bowerman was tall.

Ignatius Bowerman's rolled from side to side a bit when he was walking, which meant that even with my scarf-slash-seatbelt, I had to hold on with both hands to stop myself from slipping off his shoulder. We didn't talk much. I don't know why Ignatius Bowerman didn't talk much, but I didn't because I wanted to concentrate on looking at the things that were around me; good investigators concentrate a lot on things that might be important later in their investigations. I saw:

1. Fields that weren't organised into regular shapes like rectangles or squares.
2. Stone walls that had a few stones missing, but could probably keep sheep or cows in.
3. Sheep that ran away from a walking rock with a boy on his shoulder.
4. Cows that were asleep and didn't really notice a walking rock with a boy on his shoulder.

I couldn't think of a reason why these things might be important later in my investigation, but I remembered them anyway. I decided while I was up on Ignatius Bowerman's shoulder that he must have very long legs. I decided this because we were moving more quickly over the ground that I would have done on my own legs. I don't know how fast we were going because I wasn't looking at my map of Dartmoor, but I do now know that stone walls with a few stones missing couldn't keep Ignatius Bowerman in or out.

After ten minutes of walking-slash-riding over fields and past animals, we came to a slope of open moorland. I knew that it was open moorland because:

1. There were no more stone walls, which meant that there were no more irregular shaped fields.
2. There were lots of gorse plants.

Ignatius Bowerman took exactly thirty one steps up this hill *(he didn't mind stepping on the prickly gorse plants)* and stopped in front of a rock that was not as tall as him *(or as tall as me on his shoulders)*. After he had stopped, Ignatius Bowerman said something.

He said, "Wake up Figgie, you lazy lump. Have you been eating too much pudding again?"

Although it looked that Ignatius Bowerman the talking rock, was talking to a rock that didn't talk, I presumed that this was his brother Figgie Daniel. I presumed this because:

1. The name 'Figgie' is an unusual one.
2. I was the only other person or rock there and my name is Thomas.

I decided that this would be a good time to continue my investigation, so I used the scarf that I'd tied around Ignatius Bowerman's neck, to climb down off his shoulder and onto his knee; after that it was quite easy to slide down to the ground. It felt strange to be so low down again, and from the floor, Figgie Daniel looked much taller than he had from Ignatius Bowerman's shoulder. I looked up at the two Bowerman brothers. Ignatius was much taller than Figgie, and Figgie was much wider than Ignatius. You couldn't tell that they were brothers; in the same way that you can tell that some people are brothers. They didn't have the same hair colour, because rocks don't have hair, they didn't have the same eye colour because rocks don't have eyes, and although Figgie was covered in lichen, Ignatius was mostly bare rock.

(Lichen is a very, very short plant that grows on rocks and makes them different colours).

"Why isn't he talking to us?" I asked Ignatius Bowerman.

"Oh, it's probably just one of his childish jokes," he replied. "I told you that he was annoying. Hey Figgie, wake up, I've brought you a visitor," and with that Ignatius Bowerman patted his brother very firmly on his rock-back. I said 'patted' then, person who is reading my non-story, but I think that if Ignatius Bowerman 'patted' one of us on the back with the same amount of force, then we would have fallen over and maybe even broken some of our ribs. I made a note-in-my-head to make sure that I stepped out of the way if Ignatius Bowerman ever looked like he was going to pat me on the back. It was then that I heard the second talking rock that I've ever met, do some talking; but he didn't talk in the way that his brother did Ignatius Bowerman did. Figgie's way of talking was very different.

"Welcome to Easdon, my favourite hill; sometimes it's blustery, sometimes it's still."

"Good evening, brother," replied Ignatius Bowerman, in a grumpy voice. "Do you think that this could finally be the night when we talk in sentences, instead of in rhymes?"

Apparently the answer to this question was 'no', because Figgie Daniel replied, "Talking in rhymes is good for the soul; so that's how we do it, up here on this knoll."

"What's a 'knoll'?" I whispered to Ignatius Bowerman. "And why is he talking like that?"

Ignatius Bowerman didn't bother to whisper when he replied, "I told you that he was annoying. Ever since he has been a rock, he has refused to use sensible words and thinks that it is clever to say everything in a rhyme. A 'knoll' is a very little hill. It is not even the right word for Easdon Hill, which is quite big. Listening to

Figgie is enough to drive a sensible huntsman insane." Ignatius Bowerman patted Figgie hard on the back again. "Figgie old chap, stop being so irritating, and allow me to introduce Thomas. He wants to ask you some questions."

"Ah welcome dear Thomas, a fine young man; how good are you with a frying pan?"

"Why is he talking about frying pans?" I whispered again. "Is he hungry?" I hoped that Figgie Daniel wasn't hungry. Although I'm very good at washing up, I'm not very good at cooking; you'd be surprised at how much imagination cooking requires.

"Oh, he is always talking about food," replied Ignatius Bowerman, in a loud voice, "he's always talking about food, but he can't eat it anymore."

"Why can't he eat food anymore?"

"Dear me, Thomas, most of the time, I think that you're a very intelligent young man, but sometimes you ask the most foolish of questions. Figgie is a rock, and no rock that you or I have ever met, has been able to eat."

I wanted to reply to Ignatius Bowerman that

I'd never met a rock that was able to move, talk, laugh, cry or sigh before I'd met him; but I didn't say anything, I don't really know why.

"Talking rocks, walking rocks, those you can see; but never a rock who is eating his tea," said Figgie sadly. It wasn't clear whether he was talking to me or to his brother; but it was clear that Ignatius Bowerman had been right about two things:

1. Figgie Daniel and Ignatius Bowerman were very different.
2. Figgie Daniel was annoying.

I've tried in my English lessons to like poetry, because Mrs Aitken really loves it. You can tell by the way she holds her head to one side, and by her soft voice when she reads it out to us, that it is one of her favourite things. I've tried really hard, but poetry to me just sounds like somebody using lots of complicated words to say something really simple. Here's an example, it's the end of a poem written by somebody called Robert Frost. Mrs Aitken had one tear on her cheek when she read it:

"I shall be telling this with a sigh
Somewhere ages and ages hence:
Two roads diverged in a wood, and I,
I took the one less travelled by,
And that has made all the difference."

What Mr Frost was saying, is that when he was walking in the woods, he was pleased with the path that he chose to walk along. He used 144 words to say what I said in just 19 words. Poems are all supposed to have a deeper meaning; the deeper meaning of this one is, that we shouldn't choose to do something in our life, just because another person has chosen to do it. Again, I just said that in 19 words. I had no idea why Mr Frost chose to use 125 more words than he needed to.

I also had no idea why Figgie Daniel had chosen to say everything in a rhyme *(a rhyme is like a part of a poem)*. I don't think that he'd had a deeper meaning when he'd said, 'how good are you with a frying pan?' If he had, I hadn't understood the deeper meaning. I'd like to be able to ask Mrs Aitken about this; but if I did, she would work out that my non-story is actually a real story, and I don't want her to do that. *(I don't know why I don't want her to)*.

I decided to be polite with Figgie Daniel, even though I felt that he was being annoying. "Good evening, Mr Figgie. I hope that you're well. I'm not good at cooking, or at using a frying pan, but I'm good at investigating. I'm doing an investigation at the moment, please may I ask you a few questions?" *(I decided to call him 'Mr Figgie', because having a conversation with two rocks called 'Mr Bowerman' might have been a bit complicated)*.

"Questions are fine, they stretch your mind; they help you to learn and they help you to find," replied Figgie Daniel.

Ignatius Bowerman sighed at his brother when he said this, and took a step backwards. However, I didn't think that Figgie Daniel's reply was too annoying, so I asked another question. "I'm looking for your brother's, Ignatius Bowerman's, hounds. He can't find them, and I wondered if you had any information that might help me to investigate their current location?"

"Hounds are horrid, nasty and mean; do you know where they were last seen?"

"Thank you for your helpful answer, would it be alright to ask you some more questions." *(Figgie's answer hadn't been helpful, but I'd decided to be very, very polite to him so that he would answer my questions)*. Ignatius Bowerman obviously thought the same about the unhelpfulness of his brother's answer, because he sighed in a very huffy way, and stomped off to the top of the hill. I hoped that he wasn't going to forget about me and leave me on Easdon Hill; but I ignored his stomping and concentrated on asking Figgie Daniel questions. "Your brother last saw his hounds on Hayne Down about three hundred years ago, when he was being turned into a rock by the witches. He hasn't seen them since then. Do you know anything about their disappearance?"

"Witches, snitches, ugly cold bags; I hate every one of the smelly old hags."

This wasn't an answer to my question, but it was interesting because I now knew that both of the Bowerman brothers hated witches. *(It also seemed likely, because they had turned them into rocks, that the witches hated both of the Bowerman brothers).*

I asked a more specific question *(I like being specific).* "Please could you tell me where you last saw your brother's hounds?"

"They were running and running up onto their hill; 'til the hag bags found them and they became still."

This was a sort of answer to my question. I thought about it for forty-five seconds and decided three things:

1. Hounds are not usually still.
2. Something must have happened to them, to make them become still.
3. The witches might have turned Ignatius Bowerman's hounds into rocks.

I wasn't sure about number three it was just a suspicion. *(Having a suspicion about something is a bit like knowing about it, but it means that you could possibly be wrong)*. I'm hardly ever wrong, so I thought that my suspicion was probably right. I looked up Easdon Hill towards Ignatius Bowerman. He was sitting at the top of the hill and staring at his brother. I could just see enough in the moonlight to tell that he was unhappy; I could tell by the way that his rock-head hung forwards. I knew that he was going to look even more unhappy when I told him that I suspected that his hounds had been turned into rocks as well.

I thought about Figgie Daniel's last answer again, and my thinking made me ask another question, "Which hill were your brother's hounds running up when the 'hag bags' found them?" I thought that 'hag bags' was a silly way to say 'witches' but I wanted to keep on being polite to Figgie Daniel, so that he would continue trying to help me with my investigation.

Figgie answered, "There are tall hills and short hills here arounds; but the mutts were running up the hill of hounds."

"Hmm, the 'hill of hounds'. Can you tell me

any more about that place?" I asked.

Figgie's reply was yet another rhyme, "A hill of green and pleasant grass tracks; where huge rocks loom in awesome stacks."

I presumed that 'awesome stacks' meant that the hill where Ignatius Bowerman's hounds were had a tor on top of it. This was both helpful and not helpful, because most hills on Dartmoor have tors on top of them. Most hills on Dartmoor have grass on them too; I knew this because grass is shown as green lines on a map, and my Dartmoor map had lots of green lines on it.

I also knew that most of the tors had names, so I asked a longer question. "Mr Figgie, you stand on Easdon Hill and are a Dartmoor tor called Figgie Daniel, your brother Ignatius stands on Hayne Down and is a Dartmoor tor called Bowerman's Nose; do you know the name of the hill or the tor that you have just told me about? The one where Ignatius' hounds were turned into rocks?"

I saw Figgie Daniel move for the first time then, because he turned his head to look at me. I looked back at him. The lichen on his rock-face made it seem a bit more like a person's face than his brother's face did. The little cracks around his rock-mouth were in the sort of pattern that Mum's face lines are when she is laughing, and I wondered if he was enjoying being asked questions and answering with rhyming answers.

His next answer was, "The hill of hounds, the hill of hounds; where dogs sit atop the rocky mounds."

I was starting to feel exasperated again, so I decided to go and talk to Ignatius Bowerman, and come back to talk to Figgie later. I decided to go for two reasons:

1. I didn't want Ignatius Bowerman to forget about me and go back to Hayne Down on his own.
2. I had some bad news to tell Ignatius Bowerman about his hounds.

I was still trying to be polite to Figgie Daniel, so I said, "Thank you for your help Mr Figgie. I'm just going up the hill to talk to your brother about this, and I'll be back soon."

"Iggie and Figgie on a hill at night; will they laugh or will they fight?" Replied Figgie Daniel. I thought that this was an unusual reply; but not too silly, because one of the brothers looked like he was laughing, and the other one looked very grumpy. I turned to walk up the hill. As I walked, I heard Figgie Daniel giggling behind me.

"See you soon Thomas, funny little man; give Iggie a hug and cheer him up if you can."

I really wasn't sure what to think about Figgie Daniel. As you can imagine *(because you can do imagining)* not being sure is something that I don't do very often. I usually make decisions about things very quickly *(on average, I'd say that a decision takes me four seconds)* and I don't like changing my mind. On this occasion, I wasn't sure about Figgie Daniel, because he was a very strange rock. I know that any moving-slash-talking rock is a strange one, but Ignatius Bowerman was easier to understand than his brother; he forgot things, but he was quite a simple rock-slash-person. He loved hunting and he loved his hounds, I also think that he loved his brother, despite being annoyed by him. Figgie Daniel, on the other hand, was hard to understand. *('On the other hand' is a phrase that Mrs Aitken likes; it means a different point of view, and is actually nothing to do with hands).* Figgie Daniel had asked me to cheer his brother up, which probably meant that he cared about his brother; but he'd answered all of my investigation questions in rhyme, which I didn't think was very helpful. Especially when I knew that the actual thing that would cheer Ignatius Bowerman up would be to find his hounds. I wondered if perhaps the witches had anything to do with Figgie Daniel talking in rhyme; maybe he couldn't talk like a normal rock/person anymore. *(Not that being a rock-slash-person is at all normal).*

I reached Ignatius Bowerman, and sat down next to him on the grass.

"Hello Mr Bowerman, what are you doing up here?" I asked. I asked this because I wanted to find out if he could remember why he was on Easdon Hill looking at his brother."

"Thomas, I thought you said that you were good at remembering," he answered, "Have you forgotten that I brought you here to ask my brother Figgie some questions about my hounds?"

I laughed at this, because it was actually Ignatius Bowerman who always forgot things, and not me. *(Laughing is not something that I do very often, so I was a bit surprised that I'd done it).*

"No, Mr Bowerman. I hadn't forgotten, but I wondered if you had."

"Forgotten what?" Asked Ignatius Bowerman.

I looked at his rock-face closely; it looked a little bit like one of his rock eyes was winking at me. I couldn't be sure whether or not he'd just been teasing me when he'd said, 'forgotten what?' I also couldn't be sure whether or not Ignatius Bowerman and I were becoming friends.

The idea of friends is one that I find a bit difficult to understand. I know that friends like talking to each other, and that they enjoy doing the same things. I looked the word 'friends' up on the internet once, and it means so many different things that I got confused. As I don't really have any friends, I didn't really know whether Ignatius Bowerman was my friend or not. *(My Mum might have been my friend, but she is my Mum instead; and Mrs Aitken might have been my friend, but she is my teacher instead).*

So I asked him, "Mr Bowerman, do you think that we are friends; or are we just a boy called Thomas and a rock called Ignatius Bowerman, who are doing an investigation together?"

Ignatius Bowerman thought about this question for so long, *(ninety-two seconds, which is the same as one minute and thirty-two seconds)*, that I wasn't sure that he'd remembered what the question was by the time he replied.

But he had remembered, and he said, "Being a rock makes it difficult to make friends, Thomas. I've tried talking to a few people since the witches did this to me, but I usually scare them. There was one girl, about thirty years ago, who talked to me and said that we could be friends. She visited once or twice a year for about five years. You remind me of her. I was very sad when she stopped coming to visit."

I was interested in this girl and wanted to find out more about her, but I was more interested about whether or not Ignatius Bowerman and I were friends. He hadn't quite answered my question about this, so I decided to ask another way, "Would you like to be my friend, Mr Bowerman?"

This time Ignatius Bowerman only needed five seconds to think of his answer. "Yes, Thomas. Yes, I'd like that very much indeed. It can get very lonely being a rock with an annoying brother who only talks in rhyme, and I really miss my hounds."

I was pleased to hear Ignatius Bowerman's answer. It sounded like, despite being a boy who remembers and a rock who forgets, we were a bit similar in some important ways. It can get very lonely being a boy who is extra-ordinary and likes to listen in geography.

I asked another question, "Do you think Figgie is your friend too?"

"Figgie is my little brother, and I love him

very much. I'd do anything for him, but he talks in an annoying way, and I don't think I can be friends with someone who annoys me that much. It would appear, Thomas, that you're my only friend. I hope that you don't mind this."

"I don't mind at all," I said. "I think that you're probably my only friend as well. I've got Mum and Mrs Aitken, but they're my mum and my teacher, and I don't think that mums and teachers can be friends as well as doing their other jobs."

"You're probably right about mums and teachers. Figgie and I had a tutor, not a teacher, but he was very strict, and definitely not our friend," said Ignatius Bowerman, "If I could drink a glass of wine right now, I'd propose a toast; and my toast would be this, 'To Thomas..., what's your other name ... ?"

"My other name is Etherington. It's the same name as my Mum's, but not the same name as my Dad's, because they aren't married. I haven't got a middle name."

"That's strange, I think Etherington was

one of the names of the girl who used to come and visit me. And now my toast, 'To Thomas Etherington and Ignatius Bowerman, may they be friends for a very long time.'"

I'd heard toasts being proposed at my aunt's wedding, so I knew what I was supposed to do next. I stood up, looked straight at Ignatius Bowerman's rock-face and repeated his words, "To Thomas Etherington and Ignatius Bowerman, may they be friends for a very long time." After that, I sat down again next to my new friend, and thought about what I needed to say to him. I had two important pieces of information for him:

1. I thought that his hounds had been turned into rocks.
2. I thought that his brother could only speak in rhyme, because the witches had cast a speaking-in-rhyme spell on him.

I decided to start with the information that wouldn't make him feel too sad.

"Mr Bowerman, I have a theory about your brother. It's about him speaking in rhyme all of the time."

"I think that you should call me 'Iggie' now that we are friends, Thomas. It is what my brother calls me, and although I prefer my full name, I think friends usually use nicknames. I shall call you Tom."

This was a tricky moment for me because I really hate being called 'Tom' *(I've told you about that already)* but I didn't want to offend Ignatius Bowerman, when he was trying to be my friend.

I decided to be honest, because being honest is important when you're friends with somebody. "I hope you don't mind Mr Bowerman, but I don't like being called 'Tom' because it's not my actual name and I don't like nicknames. I prefer you calling me 'Thomas', maybe I could call you 'Ignatius'?"

What Ignatius Bowerman said next, showed me he didn't mind. "That's fine by me Thomas, you can call me whatever you'd like to, because you're my friend. I'd be interested to hear the theory that you just mentioned about my brother; because Figgie's rhymes really annoy me, and being annoyed with him means I don't come to visit him very often."

"Right then, I shall call you Ignatius from now on," I replied, "Ignatius, my theory is that Figgie isn't talking in rhymes to annoy you; he's talking in rhymes because the witches cast a spell on him that means that he can't talk any other way."

"That is indeed an interesting theory," said Ignatius Bowerman, "you could well be correct; I don't recall Figgie ever talking in rhymes before he was turned into a rock. He liked reading poetry, but he didn't make his own rhymes up."

"Well maybe that's why he talks in such good rhymes now," I suggested, "someone who likes reading poetry would be good at making up rhymes, because lots of poems have rhymes in them."

"I think your theory might be correct, Thomas, it might be correct, and it makes me feel better. It makes me feel better, because it will help me to stop being annoyed with Figgie all of the time. He is, after all, the only brother that I have."

I was pleased that Ignatius Bowerman liked my theory, but I'd something else to tell him, that I didn't think he would like so much. "I've another theory for you, Ignatius, but I don't think that you will like this one."

"I trust you, Thomas, you're my friend. I'm sure that you would not tell me something that I did not like unless you thought that I needed to hear it."

"I do think that you need to hear this Ignatius. It's a theory about your hounds; my investigation suggests that they might have been turned into rock by the witches, on the same night that you and Figgie were."

Ignatius Bowerman was silent after I'd said this. He was silent for twenty-four seconds, and then he said, "My dear friend Thomas, I'm deeply saddened to hear that my beautiful, fierce hounds might have been turned into cold, solid rock; but I'd still like to know where they are. Did Figgie give you any useful information about their whereabouts?"

Ignatius Bowerman didn't cry about my theory, but he did look very unhappy. "I'm sorry that my second theory has made you sad, Ignatius. Figgie only spoke to me in rhyme, but he did mention a hill that sounded like it would be the place that your hounds are. His rhyme said, '*A hill of green and pleasant grass tracks; where huge rocks loom in awesome stacks.*' and he also said, '*The hill of hounds, the hill of hounds; where dogs sit atop the rocky mounds.*' Have you ever been anywhere that might fit his descriptions?"

"I think I've been many places that fit his descriptions," replied Ignatius Bowerman, "as you know, I'm not very good at remembering. If only we had a map to help us."

And then I did some remembering of my own; I had a map of Dartmoor with me, in my fleece pocket. I patted my tummy, it was still there and so was the torch.

"I've got a map of Dartmoor right here, Ignatius. Would you like to look at it with me?"

"That's an excellent idea, Thomas, but it is quite dark at the moment, will we be able to see the map properly?"

"We will be able to see the map properly, Ignatius, because I'm a very organised investigator, and I've remembered to bring a torch."

I put the map on the grass, so that both of us could see the area of Dartmoor that we were sitting in.

I shone the torch onto the map. "Can you see Ignatius? I'm shining the torch on Easdon Hill, which is where we two friends are both sitting now." Then I shone the torch onto another place on the map, just south of Easdon Hill *(on a map, south is always down)*. "And can you see here Ignatius? Now I'm shining the torch on Hayne Down, which is where I live and you usually stand."

Ignatius Bowerman leant forwards so that his rock-eyes were closer to the map. "Hmm, yes Thomas, I can see both Easdon Hill and Hayne Down. It is very interesting to see these places on a map, but we know that my hounds are not at either of them, because we've been there, and have failed to find them."

"You're right Ignatius," I replied, "We don't need to look at Easdon Hill and Hayne Down, we need to look on the map for somewhere that might fit your brother's description. Somewhere that has grass and high rocks and is something to do with hounds." As I said that, I moved the torch slowly around the part of the map that had Easdon Hill and Hayne Down on it, and I noticed something interesting; the map was divided into three main background colours. There were green areas that showed trees and forests, there were white areas that showed roads and fields and there were yellowish areas that showed not very much at all. Both Easdon Hill and Hayne Down were in yellowish areas, so I estimated *(I don't like guessing)* that these were areas of moorland.

"Look, Ignatius," I said to my new rock-friend, "I think your hounds must be on one of the yellowish areas of the map, because those areas have grass and rocks." As I said this, I moved the torch backwards and forwards between Easdon Hill and Hayne Down."

"You're going to have to help me with this, Thomas," said Ignatius Bowerman, "since I've been a rock, I've not been able to see any colours; everything on your map looks grey to me. I can see some place names though. Do you think that my hounds could be at Honeybag Tor?"

I moved the torch down the map until it was shining straight onto Honeybag Tor. Honeybag Tor was two kilometres south west of Hayne Down. "I don't know, they could be. It doesn't sound like a very hound-like place though. Did your hounds eat honey?"

"Thomas, for an intelligent investigator friend, sometimes you do ask very silly questions. Of course my hounds didn't eat honey. Figgie ate lots and lots of honey, but my fierce and brave hounds liked raw meat and eggs. If they'd eaten honey, they would have been fat and lazy like Figgie; but I needed them to stay fierce and brave, so I gave them lots of meat to eat."

I was a bit cross at the suggestion that my questions were silly; but I knew that friends weren't supposed to get cross with each other, so I didn't say anything else about honey. I just shone my torch a bit further south on the map. "There are some other places near to Honeybag Tor, Ignatius. Chinkwell Tor, Bell Tor, Bonehill Down, Bonehill Rocks..." I stopped speaking then, because both Bonehill Down and Bonehill Rocks sounded like places that hounds might like to go.

Ignatius Bowerman had obviously had the same thought as me because his voice sounded excited. *(Please don't ask me to describe what an excited rock-voice sounds like; I am not very good at describing).* "Bonehill Down and Bonehill Rocks? My hounds definitely liked bones. I often gave them one to fight over at bedtime. Fighting over bones kept them fierce and brave."

I didn't like the idea of hounds fighting, but that bit of information wasn't important to my investigation, so I ignored it. *(Ignoring is when you try to forget something. I'm not very good at ignoring because I'm too good at remembering).* "Your brother's rhymes talked about 'huge rocks' and 'rocky mounds', so maybe Bonehill Rocks is the next place that we need to go to."

"That sounds like good thinking Thomas, but I don't know how to find Bonehill Rocks. I've probably been there before, but I'm sorry to say that I cannot remember the occasion."

"You don't need to worry about finding Bonehill Rocks, Ignatius," I replied, "We have a map and a torch. I'll sit on your shoulder and I'll be the navigator."

"That sounds like an excellent plan, Thomas. Would you like to climb up onto my shoulder now? While I'm sitting down?"

Ignatius Bowerman's idea was a good one. I folded the map so that I could still see Easdon Hill, Hayne Down and Bonehill Rocks, and pushed it and the torch back into my fleece pocket. Then I climbed onto Ignatius Bowerman's knees and pulled myself up onto his shoulder. I tied my scarf back around me and then I said, "I'm ready Ignatius. Do you want to go and say goodbye to Figgie before we go?"

"I suppose it would be a good idea to say goodbye to him, but I daresay he will probably be annoying and answer in a rhyme," answered Ignatius Bowerman.

It only took five of Ignatius Bowerman's giant steps for us to get back down the hill to Figgie Daniel. I was used to the side-to-side motion of my rock-ride by now and was happy to back up so high.

Figgie sounded pleased to see us again. "Ah, Thomas and Iggie, there you both are; sometimes you're near, but most times you're far."

Ignatius Bowerman just huffed and shrugged his shoulders at this rhyme greeting; so I said, "Mr Figgie, we've both come to say thank you for all of your help with our hound investigation, and to say 'bye' for now. I hope that we'll be able to come back again soon to visit you, but now my friend Ignatius and I have to go and look for his hounds."

Figgie Daniel opened his lichen-rock-eyes at this news, and looked straight at his brother. "Iggie, Iggie Iggie, has lost his hounds; I hope they're to be found among Dartmoor's mounds."

"Thank you, Mr Figgie, that's a very kind thing

to say, because your brother, my friend, misses his hounds very much." I stopped speaking for a moment and nudged Ignatius Bowerman's rock-neck hard with my elbow. When he didn't speak, I nudged him again and said, "Don't you, Ignatius?" in a meaningful voice. *('Meaningful' means something that has lots of hidden messages linked to it. In this case, I really meant to say, 'stop being such a grumpy rock and say thank you to your brother').*

I knew that Ignatius Bowerman didn't want to talk to Figgie Daniel, and I was relieved when he did. "Indeed, yes, thank you very much, my brother. It has been a pleasure to visit you again, and the information that you gave Thomas has been most useful."

"Down-faced brother, come again soon; we'll sit and talk under the moon," replied Figgie Daniel.

I was pleased to hear that, despite all of Ignatius Bowerman's grumpiness, Figgie Daniel still wanted to see his brother again. If you only have one brother and one friend, like Ignatius

Bowerman, then it's important to make sure that you see both of them as often as possible.

I decided to try to say goodbye to Figgie Daniel with a rhyme of my own. *(I'm going to trust you here, person who is reading my non-story, not to laugh at my very bad rhyme)*. "Goodbye and thanks, tall Mr Figgie; you haven't got hair, where is your wiggie?" I knew that 'wiggie' wasn't a real word, but the only other word that I could think of to rhyme with 'Figgie' was 'Iggie' and my friend and I had already agreed that I wouldn't use his nickname.

Figgie Daniel obviously thought that my rhyme was funny because he laughed a rock-laugh and said, "You need rhyming practice, Thomas the clown; have fun with my brother, back on Hayne Down."

I knew he was right about me needing rhyming practice, but I also knew that I wasn't going to do any rhyming practice, because I actually found rhymes as annoying as my friend Ignatius Bowerman did. Something else I knew was that, although he hadn't said anything about my very bad rhyme, Ignatius Bowerman had also thought that it was funny. I knew this for two reasons:

1. As he turned to carry me back down the hill, I could feel his shoulders moving up and down, in a laughing sort of movement.

2. Just before we got to the bottom of Easdon Hill, Ignatius Bowerman turned his head around and shouted, "Goodbye Wiggie. My clown and I are off to find my hounds."

I didn't really like being called a 'clown' by two brothers who weren't even people anymore.

(Clowns are men who wear ridiculous make-up and scare young boys in their pushchairs, when the boys' mothers have taken them to the fair. I definitely wasn't a clown and would much rather have been called an investigator or a scientist. I didn't say anything about that though because I thought that it was probably good for two brothers to share a joke about something; even if that something was me).

I checked my adventure watch with the camouflage strap, I'd estimated that it was midnight and I was nearly right, my watch told me that it was five minutes past midnight. Ignatius Bowerman and I still had plenty of time to do some more hound investigation before I needed to get home, to my bed, in my bedroom, in my house, on Hayne Down.

Nine
Natsworthy

It was now thirteen minutes past midnight and if I had been Cinderella, my carriage would have turned into a pumpkin by this time. As I was not Cinderella *(because she was an invented girl)*, and my carriage was in fact a man who had already turned into something strange; I knew that it was safe to carry on with our investigation. We needed to do two important things:

1. Find Bonehill Rocks.
2. Find out if Ignatius Bowerman's hounds were at Bonehill Rocks.

Up until that moment, *(the moment when I was riding on Ignatius Bowerman's shoulder past a place called Barracott Farm)*, I'd known that I was good at investigating, and I'd known that I really wanted to find the hounds, but I hadn't known if we were actually going to find them. As we passed Barracott Farm, I thought that it was more likely that we would find them than we wouldn't. This thought made me feel excited and, despite it being after midnight, I didn't feel sleepy at all.

I think that Ignatius Bowerman was having the same thoughts as me, because he was moving much faster than he had been before. His bigger strides were causing two problems:

1. They were making him move from side to side so much that I was nearly falling off.
2. I wasn't sure that he was taking them in the right direction.

"Excuse me, Ignatius," I decided to be polite again. "Would you mind slowing down a bit? I'm finding it difficult to stay on your shoulder."

"Oh, I do apologise Thomas. I was so excited about finding my hounds, that I'd quite forgotten that you were up there," said Ignatius Bowerman.

I shouldn't really have been surprised at this, because since I'd met my new friend Ignatius Bowerman, he'd forgotten about lots of things. But I was surprised, because I knew that if I had someone sitting on my shoulder, I'd notice that he *(or she)* was there because people, even partly grown ones, are quite heavy.

"Please try to remember that I'm here, Ignatius," I said. "I'm your friend, and friends should not forget about each other. Have you remembered the way to Bonehill Rocks?"

"Bonehill Rocks?" Ignatius Bowerman sounded surprised. "I've never even heard of Bonehill Rocks. Are you sure that you haven't imagined them? Bonehill seems like a strange name for some rocks. I'm taking you to Hayne Down, where you live, and I usually stand."

"I can't have imagined them, because I don't do imagining," I said crossly *(even though I knew that you shouldn't be cross with friends)*, "We're going to Bonehill Rocks, because your brother Figgie Daniel told us a rhyme about where your hounds are; and it sounded a bit like Bonehill

Rocks could be the place that he was rhyming about."

"Ah, Figgie. I've not seen the funny old fella in a very long time. How is he?"

I tried to sound patient when I explained, "You have just seen him, Ignatius. He was fine, but you were grumpy with him, because he was talking in rhymes all of the time."

"You're a cheeky young man Thomas, even though you're my friend," Ignatius Bowerman said, "I resent the suggestion that I was grumpy, it cannot possibly be true. I'm a hunter, and I'm known for being jovial and friendly."

Because I was finding being patient difficult, I wanted to tell Ignatius Bowerman that he wasn't a hunter anymore, and that he was just a rock; but I thought that this might upset him, and not help us to find his hounds, so I didn't say those things.

Instead I said, "We need to go to Bonehill Rocks, not to Hayne Down. Please could you wait a minute, while I get my map and torch out?"

Ignatius Bowerman seemed to have already forgotten about his forgetting. "Of course I'll wait Thomas, friends are supposed to wait for each other. Please could you hurry up though, because I'd like to find my hounds soon."

I knew it wouldn't take me long to choose a route, because we only needed to go four kilometres. I shone the torch onto the map. Since we'd left Figgie Daniel, we'd come down off Easdon Hill and followed a farm track to the road. It had been difficult following the farm track, because it was narrow, and Ignatius Bowerman was wide; sometimes he'd had to turn sideways to squeeze past the hedges, and he still had bits of hedge plants attached to him. I knew that we'd just gone past Barracott, because I'd seen a sign that said, 'Barracott Farm'. Because of these things, it was quite easy to find exactly where we were on the map. After running my finger along two different possible routes to Bonehill Rocks, I choose the one that would **not** take us over Hayne Down and past my house. I choose this one because:

1. I didn't want Ignatius Bowerman *(and maybe me)* to get tangled up with the trees again.
2. I thought that if we went past the place where he usually stood, Ignatius Bowerman might forget what we were doing *(again!)* and just do standing instead.

The route that I'd chosen took us past a place called Natsworthy Manor. I thought that Natsworthy Manor sounded important enough for Ignatius Bowerman to have heard of it.

So I asked him, "Ignatius my friend, do you know how to find a place called Natsworthy Manor?"

"Old Natsworthy, eh?" Replied Ignatius Bowerman. "Now he was a queer fellow. He fancied himself as a grand hunter, but the only things that he could catch were pigeons. Whenever we went for supper at Natsworthy Manor, the only thing on the menu was pigeon pie. Figgie didn't like it there because there was never any pudding."

I laughed at Ignatius Bowerman's answer.

Pigeon pie didn't sound that tasty and I wondered if they took the feathers off before baking it. "Do you think you could find your way to Natsworthy Manor from here?"

"Oh yes, that would be easy for me. Figgie and I used to wander around these lanes all the time when we were boys. We used to play in the streams and climb trees in the woods."

It was interesting to think about Ignatius Bowerman and Figgie Daniel playing together when they were young, I wondered what they had looked like. It was interesting, but I didn't have time to think about it then, because we needed to find Bonehill Rocks. "Do you think you could take me there, Ignatius. It's about half way to Bonehill Rocks, where I think your hounds might be."

"In that case, I'll take you to Natsworthy straight away. I don't suppose the old man lives there anymore; he was at least a hundred years old when I knew him! Hold tight, Thomas, I'll try not to go too fast."

Now that Ignatius Bowerman had slowed

down, it was again fun riding along on his shoulder. This lane was bigger than the farm track, but he still nearly filled it, and I was relieved that it was midnight and not midday. If someone had seen us, I don't think that either of us would have been able to explain a rock that was supposed to be on Hayne Down, walking along a road near to Natsworthy Manor, with a boy on his shoulder. The only thing that did see us was a fox, which stood in the middle of the lane, stared for fifteen seconds and then went off across a field. I concluded from this, that foxes are probably less easy to shock than people.

When you drive along Devon lanes in a car, it's quite boring *(and difficult to play 'I-Spy')* because the hedges are too green and high for you to see over them. When you ride along Devon lanes on a rock's shoulder, it is not at all boring because, even if it is dark, you can see quite a long way over the hedges. The moon was still bright and much higher in the sky now, so I could see some fields and beyond them, some dark shadowy trees. I also saw Natsworthy Manor before we got to it; this was because there were some lights on in the upstairs windows.

I was expecting a house that was called 'Manor' to be much bigger and grander than the one that I saw from Ignatius Bowerman's shoulder. This house was bigger than my house, but it still looked like a house to me and not a 'manor'. I made a note in my head to use the internet to find out what exactly 'manor' meant. Natsworthy Manor was a grey building, with tiles all the way down the front of it. It had white window frames that held in little square panes of glass, and tall grey chimneys. Grey houses do not often look like they're cosy inside, but this one did, I think it was because of the way the light shone in slightly different directions through each pane of glass. I could tell that Ignatius Bowerman had seen the Manor, and the lights too, because he was walking more slowly, and had turned his head to look at it.

"The Manor house is smaller than I remember it being," he said. "Thomas, can you see the top window on the right, next to the arbour? Well, that's where Figgie and I used to climb out at night, when we wanted to explore in the dark. We didn't have Father's permission to do this, but when he and his hunting friends had finished eating pigeon pie and started drinking, we were often told to go upstairs to 'play'. They drank far too much to remember to check what two boys were up to."

When I heard that, I decided that if Ignatius Bowerman and I had been boys at the same time and not over three hundred years apart, then we would have had a good time together because we enjoy some of the same things.

(Although I wouldn't enjoy hunting because I'm a vegetarian and he wouldn't enjoy internet searching because he probably doesn't even know what a computer is).

"It seems like quite a small manor house to me." I said, "But I don't know very much about manor houses. Did you live in one, or did you live in a castle?"

"There you go, being silly again, Thomas," Ignatius Bowerman replied, "Huntsmen never live in castles, they always live in manor houses. You must know that, or maybe things have changed; where do huntsmen live nowadays?"

I thought about this question for fourteen seconds. It was a difficult one to answer, but I did my best. "I don't know where huntsmen live now, because we don't really have huntsmen anymore. People go hunting sometimes, but it isn't their job. They usually have jobs like judges and teachers and policemen; hunting is their hobby."

Ignatius Bowerman was puzzled. "Thomas, please could you explain what a hobby is. I don't know that word."

"Of course I can Ignatius," I replied, trying to be helpful, "A hobby is an activity that you really like doing, and you do quite a lot, but you don't get paid to do it. For example, at the moment, my hobbies are searching for information on the internet, and talking to rocks."

"I don't know what the internet is, Thomas, but talking to rocks sounds like a very rewarding hobby to me," said Ignatius Bowerman, "I think though, that you're misunderstanding my family situation somewhat. My father wasn't just a hunter; he had a responsibility to look after all of the people who lived on his land. He had to make sure that they had enough to eat and sort out their arguments. He was always very busy. I suppose you could say that hunting was his hobby. It was my hobby as well, I do not recall having another job, though."

"Well I am pretty sure that we both have a job at the moment," I reminded him, "My job is to investigate the whereabouts of your hounds, and your job is to take me to where we need to go to do the investigating. When I look at the map, I can see that we need to go a bit further down this road, then straight up the hill to Honeybag Tor and along to Bonehill Rocks."

"I'm very sorry, Thomas, but I think that I've forgotten something important. Why are we going to Bonehill Rocks? It sounds like a strange place."

I sighed, but not too loudly because at least this time, Ignatius Bowerman had noticed that he'd forgotten something. "We're going to Bonehill Rocks because your brother, Figgie Daniel, said some things that made us think that your hounds might be there."

"Ah, I see. Well, why are we standing still outside this old manor house then?" asked Ignatius Bowerman. "Let's make an immediate departure, Thomas. We must go as quick as the wind. I'd like to see my hounds at Bonehill Rocks."

"You're right Ignatius," I said tactfully. *(Tactfully is a way of saying something that makes the other person/rock feel happy, but doesn't say what you actually want to say. Mum says that I should practise being tactful).* "I don't know why we're standing here. We do need to go down the lane, and find Bonehill Rocks."

Ten
Stuck in a Bog

It didn't take long at all to get along the lane to the bottom of the hill that had Honeybag Tor on it. It was quite a steep slope up to the tor, and a boy on his own would have been out of breath by the time he got there. A boy sitting on a rock's shoulder, however, was not out of breath at all, and neither was the rock. This meant that we could have a conversation standing on top of the sloping grey stacks of rock on Honeybag Tor. I could see that they were grey, because the moon was still bright.

"Are you excited, Ignatius?" I asked my rock-friend. "We might be very near to your hounds now."

"I'm in a state of excited anticipation, Thomas," replied Ignatius Bowerman, "I haven't seen my hounds for three hundred years, and I miss them terribly."

"I don't miss your hounds, Ignatius Bowerman, because I've never met them; but I'd really like to meet them. Especially Rocky, he sounds like the sort of hound that I'd like to spend time with."

What I didn't know then, but I know now *(this is called hindsight)*, was that if it had been day-time and the sun had been shining straight on us, instead of on the moon, both Ignatius Bowerman and I would have been able to see exactly where his hounds were, from the place where we were standing on top of Honeybag Tor. I'm not going to tell you exactly where they were yet, because I want you to be really keen to read the next part of my non-story. Mrs Aitken once told our English class that these 'make-people-keen-to-read-your-story' sentences are called 'cliffhangers'. There are only rocks and no cliffs in my non-story, but despite that, I think that I've just written a cliffhanger.

I looked at the map again, Bonehill Rocks was very near, and I was sure that I was going to be able to show Ignatius Bowerman what a great investigator I was, and find his hounds for him. I think I should tell you now, person who is reading my non-story, that I wasn't right about this; I wasn't right, and the next part of my non-story will tell you how I found this out.

Before we went any further, I decided *(or, my body decided)* that I needed to do something important. This something important wasn't to do with me looking for hounds, although it was something that hounds do a lot. This something important was that I needed to pee. My body deciding this was a tricky moment for me, because although Ignatius Bowerman was now my friend, I was still a bit shy about telling him what I needed to do. I've noticed, by the way, that lots of ordinary boys, who are the same age as me, are not at all shy about telling everybody that they need to pee. They use lots of different words for it and some of the words, are ones that my mum has told me not to say. Sometimes these boys like to tell people that they need to pee, whilst they're actually having a pee, which is a bit silly, because anybody who is looking at them peeing knows that they need it, because they're actually doing it. I don't listen and I don't look. I don't want to know who is peeing, and I don't want to tell people about me peeing. I thought about my problem for three seconds *(when you need to pee you need to think quickly)*. On Dartmoor, the usual thing for a boy to do would be to pee against a rock. I was sitting on a rock but that rock was also my friend, and I didn't think that it would be a good idea to pee on my friend. So I had to say something to Ignatius Bowerman.

I said, "Excuse me Ignatius, I know that you're in a state of excited anticipation, but I need to get down off your shoulder for a short time."

"Oh, Thomas," Ignatius Bowerman replied, "I wish you hadn't said that, because I'm in a hurry to get to Bonehill Rocks and find my hounds.

Could you possibly get down off my shoulder when we get there, instead?"

I hunched over to try and stop the pee feeling, and I sighed, "Ignatius, I'm very sorry, but I can't wait until we get to Bonehill Rocks. I've got an urgent need, please could you kneel down, so I can get off your shoulder."

Ignatius Bowerman obviously didn't understand what my 'urgent need' was, and he obviously didn't think that he should take any notice of me, because he started walking again.

"I'll kneel down and let you get off my shoulder, when we get to Bonehill Rocks, Thomas. I trust that I'm heading in the right direction?" he said, "Please can you tell me when we get there?"

I didn't say anything. I didn't say anything for two reasons:

1. I was very cross with Ignatius Bowerman and Mum has taught me to wait until I'm just a medium bit cross, before I talk to people.

2. I was concentrating very hard on not peeing on Ignatius Bowerman's shoulder.

Ignatius Bowerman was walking quite fast again. In one way, this was good news for me, because it was clear that he wasn't going to let me get down until we got to Bonehill Rocks. As well as being good news for me, this was also bad news for me, because going fast over the bumpy grass made him joggle around even more than he had along the lane; and joggling is not something that any boy wants to do when he is desperate for a pee. I used the word 'desperate' then, because I really was feeling it. Even if I'd decided that I didn't mind peeing on a joggling rock that was also my friend; it would have been impossible to stand up, organise my clothes and have my pee without falling off the joggling-rock-friend. I crossed my legs, hunched over a bit more and hoped that we would get there soon.

There are two tors between Honeybag Tor and Bonehill Rocks. It took Ignatius Bowerman *(and me, because I was on his shoulder)* two minutes to get to Chinkwell Tor, and one minute to get to Bell Tor. This was more good news, and I started to think that I'd be able to wait until we got to Bonehill Rocks after all. But then we hit a problem.

(The last sentence doesn't mean that we actually hit anything. It's a metaphor. Mrs Aitken taught us that a metaphor is some words that don't make actual sense; but you use them to make the meaning of something stronger. I hope she likes mine because I find metaphors difficult to understand, and really wanted to put one into my non-story).

The problem that we hit *(but didn't actually hit)* was that just below Bell Tor, there was a Dartmoor bog. Dartmoor has lots of bogs, they're usually green and look like land, until you step on them, when they wobble like a lime jelly and make you sink. They don't smell fresh like lime jelly, they smell like rotten vegetables and stinky feet. I've done some internet research into bogs because people sometimes die in them; the bodies of these people are preserved, and very interesting for forensic scientists to dissect *(I've told you already that I want to be a forensic scientist).* When I was doing my research, I found out that Dartmoor bogs are so well known that a man named Arthur Conan Doyle once wrote a story about one of them. The story is called, 'The Hound of the Baskervilles', which is a strange coincidence because my non-story is about hounds too.

If you can imagine *(I can't do imagining but you probably can)* walking around Dartmoor at night, walking into a bog and sinking down in it; then you can probably also imagine what would happen to a heavy rock with a boy on his shoulder who walked into a Dartmoor bog. I don't need to imagine this because I was actually there when it happened. That is, I didn't sink into the bog myself but I did feel it, hear it and smell it, when Ignatius Bowerman's rock-legs sank into the bog up to his knees. It felt a bit like that funny feeling in your stomach, when someone drives a car fast over a bump; it sounded a bit like the squelch of a wellington boot in mud and it smelt a lot like rotten eggs. The gas that comes from rotten eggs is hydrogen sulphide, which is also the gas that comes from farts. All of this bog sinking meant that my problem had just got bigger; I was stuck, needing a pee, on a rock, who was also stuck, in a fart-smelling bog.

At first I didn't understand that we were stuck in a bog. So I asked Ignatius Bowerman, "Why have we stopped, Ignatius? I thought that you were in a hurry to get to Bonehill Rocks." I didn't mention why I was also in a hurry, because I didn't want to talk about why.

Ignatius Bowerman was too busy moving his stuck legs up and down to answer me. "I think we..." *lift, squirm*, "... are maybe..." *lift, squirm*, "... stuck in a bog," he said, as he squelched his legs up and down. "This is not a good thing to happen at all, Thomas. Dartmoor bogs are very dangerous, I lost a hound puppy in a bog once, he sank right in. He didn't have a name, but I called him 'Bog Dog' after that, and I used to threaten the other hounds that they would end up like Bog Dog, if they failed to listen to me. It would be very ironic if I ended up like Bog Dog myself, but I think that I'm going to."

Ignatius Bowerman's rock-voice started to get higher as he spoke, and he was wriggling himself deeper and deeper into the bog. I realised that he was starting to panic; I wasn't panicking for two reasons:

1. Because I was more worried about needing to pee than sinking into a bog.
2. Because I knew that panicking in bogs is a very bad idea.

I've already told you that I'm a good internet researcher, and when I'd been finding things out about Dartmoor bogs, I'd read some information about how to get out of them. I'd found out that there are five things you should do to get out of a bog, I thought about whether we were doing the five things or not, they were:

1. Avoid getting into a bog in the first place. *(Too late for that one)*.
2. Don't panic. *(I wasn't, but Ignatius Bowerman was)*.
3. Assess the situation. *(I was doing that, but Ignatius Bowerman wasn't)*.
4. Get help. *(There wasn't anyone else there)*.
5. Move slowly. *(Ignatius Bowerman was squelching around quickly and I was not moving at all)*.

I decided that because I knew the five-bog-things and because Ignatius Bowerman was still panicking; it should be me that took charge of the situation. *(Taking charge of a situation means that you tell everyone else what to do, and sort the problem out).*

So I said in my best calm voice *(which was tricky because I was just about bursting for a pee by then)*, "Mr Bowerman," I said, 'Mr Bowerman' because I was about to say something very important, and I wanted to get his attention, "I'm an expert on getting out of bogs and you need to listen to me very carefully." This was partly a lie of course; reading about something on the internet is not the same thing as being an expert in it. But I needed to make sure that Ignatius Bowerman was going to listen to me straight away."

He didn't listen to me straight away, instead he carried on struggling and trying to lift up his legs. "I'll listen to you, Thomas, but I really do not like it in this bog, and I cannot even remember why I'm here, and not on Hayne Down."

"That is excellent news about the listening," I said, ignoring the other things. "What I want you to do first, is to stop panicking."

"Now see here, young Thomas." Now Ignatius Bowerman sounded angry as well as panicky, "I'm not panicking; I'm a hunter, and hunters never panic." And with that, I felt another downward lurch as he sank up to his rock-waist in the bog. The farty hydrogen sulphide smell of the bog went straight up my nostrils, and I put my left hand over my mouth to stop the smell, and held on tightly to my scarf with my right hand, to stop me from falling off. The smell of the green, spongy bog made me feel sick and I really didn't want to end up in it.

I also didn't want to have an argument with my sinking rock-friend, because I knew that Ignatius Bowerman could get grumpy and a grumpy, panicking rock would be even harder to reason with than a non-grumpy panicking rock. "I can see now that you aren't panicking, Ignatius." *(When I said this, I knew that it was another lie; but I think you will understand why*

I said it). "Please could you do the following things for me. Number 1 – take some deep, slow breaths. Number 2 – think carefully about what is happening. Number 3 – stop moving around so much."

"I **can** see that you still think I'm panicking, and I'm definitely not," said Ignatius Bowerman huffily, "but I've a deep desire to get out of this bog and find my hounds, so I'll do what you suggest." He stopped speaking then, and he stopped splashing around, and I could feel his rock-chest moving as he took the deep, slow breaths that I'd asked him to.

"Thank you very much for doing that, Ignatius," I said calmly into his rock-ear, "now can you see that you have stopped sinking?"

"I can see that I've stopped sinking into this infernal bog," replied Ignatius Bowerman, sounding slightly less cross, "I can also see that the reason that I've stopped sinking into it is, because I've stopped moving around so much. I've said before, Thomas, that I think that you're a very clever young man; and you've proved it once again. But one thing is puzzling me."

I was relieved that Ignatius Bowerman wasn't sinking anymore, but being relieved about that made me remember how desperate I was for a pee. Whatever the thing was that was puzzling Ignatius Bowerman, we needed to get it talked about, and get out of the bog quickly.

Which is, I think, why my voice sounded a bit strained and squeaky when I asked, "What is it that is puzzling you, Ignatius?"

"I'm puzzled about why you're jiggling around so much when you're an intelligent boy, who is sitting on my shoulder, who has just asked me to 'stop moving around'."

I found myself in a quandary then.

(A 'quandary' is a word that is tricky to spell, but when you do spell it right, it means a situation where you have to make a difficult decision).

I was in a quandary because I, in equal amounts, really needed to pee and really didn't want to tell Ignatius Bowerman that I needed to pee. I don't know if you, person who is reading my non-story, have ever been in the situation that I found myself in then. I don't mean, of course, that you might once have been sitting on a moving-slash-talking rock's shoulder, in the middle of a Dartmoor bog, at night-time, needing to pee. I mean that I don't know if you have ever needed to pee so much, that the only way to stop the pee from coming out is to jiggle around. I hope that you have, and that you understand, and aren't laughing at me, like the boys at school did in year five.

I was jiggling too much to think about my quandary for more than twenty seconds. Twenty seconds wasn't long enough to solve my problem, and the thought of peeing filled my head, so in the end, I did the only thing that I could think of doing. Holding tightly onto my scarf, I pulled myself to my feet, pulled down my jogging bottoms a bit and peed out as far away from Ignatius Bowerman as I could. In the silence of the night, my pee hitting the bog sounded as loud as a steam train as it pulls into a station. It would have been stupid of me to hope that Ignatius Bowerman wouldn't notice me peeing, because I knew that he wasn't deaf.

So I apologised to my rock friend once again. "I'm very, very sorry, Ignatius." I said as the pee streamed out of me, hit the bog and splashed onto his rock-tummy. I'm very sorry and very embarrassed." Ignatius Bowerman didn't say anything at all at this, and I was just thinking that he must be very cross with me when I realised that I'd something more important to think about. Ignatius Bowerman was shaking.

I've already said why shaking when you're stuck in a bog isn't a good idea. I didn't understand why Ignatius Bowerman was doing it, because he knew that he needed to stand still. I finished my pee, did my zip up, and sat back down on his shoulder.

And then I said to him, "Ignatius, I wish you would stay still. We still have to get out of this stinking bog, and shaking like that might make us sink into it some more."

He didn't stop shaking and I was glad that I was still holding onto my scarf. Eventually, after forty seconds more of being shaken around, I realised that Ignatius Bowerman was laughing.

"Ho, ho, ho Thomas, that is the funniest thing I've seen in three hundred years. You just stood up on my shoulder and piddled. It reminds me of the good old days. Figgie and I used to piddle out of our bedroom window and try to confuse the gardener into thinking that it was raining."

I didn't think that me getting so desperate for a pee was that funny. It may have been a bit amusing but I'd been very embarrassed about it; however, as Ignatius Bowerman kept on shaking, laughing and muttering the words, '*boy*', '*shoulder*' and '*splash*' to himself, I began to see that our situation was quite funny. People say that laughter is infectious. This is not true because laughter isn't an organism that flows around in the air and gives you diseases; but it is true that when someone else is laughing, you quite often want to laugh yourself. *(Except when lots of people are laughing **at** you; then you might want to cry instead)*. If I had wanted to, I could have said that laughter was infectious that night, because I did eventually see that it was funny, and soon my rock-friend Ignatius Bowerman and I were laughing and laughing and laughing about me standing on his shoulder, and peeing into a Dartmoor bog.

I was so busy laughing that I didn't notice how long we were doing it for. Eventually when we stopped, I put my arm round my rock-friend's neck and said, "Ignatius, that was the best laughing that I've done for a long time. Thank you very much indeed."

"The pleasure was mine, young Thomas. There is nothing like a good belly laugh with a good friend, and you're certainly a good friend. Now, let us find a way out of this bog and over to Bonehill Rocks, before daylight arrives."

I looked at my green adventure watch with the camouflage strap. "We definitely need to get out of this bog," I said, "it is six minutes past two already, we don't want to run out of time." I thought about the bog problem for thirteen seconds. As well as the 'move slowly if you're in a bog' instruction that I'd read on the internet, I'd also watched a video about a man called

'Bear Grylls' *(which isn't his real name but sounds tougher than 'Edward Michael Grylls, which is what he is really called)* who jumped into a bog just to show people how to get out of it again. Personally, I think that this was just showing off, but nonetheless, I was grateful that night that his video had shown me what we needed to do. *(Nonetheless is three short words joined into one word that in my sentence means; just because he was showing off doesn't mean that he didn't teach me something useful. I hope Mrs Aitken will be pleased that I've used it).*

"Ignatius, what you need to do to get out of the bog, is to move very slowly and try your best to pull just one of your legs up and out of it." I advised.

"That sounds quite difficult Thomas," replied Ignatius Bowerman, but I trust you because you're my friend and I really don't like bogs. "Hold on tight!" As he said this, I felt my rock-friend lean slowly over to the left, I could feel myself slipping, so I put both my arms around his rock-neck, so that I didn't slide into the bog.

"That's it Ignatius!" I said. I could see that the top of his right rock-leg was starting to pull out of the bog. "Keep pulling it out slowly."

Pulling such a big leg out was obviously an effort for my rock-friend because he was breathing deeply when he said, "I'm worried about you falling in, Thomas, I think I'm going to have to get right onto my front to get my leg out."

"It's okay," I reassured him, "that's exactly the right thing to do. Bear Grylls said so. If you move slowly enough, I can climb onto your back as you go forwards."

"Have you been talking to bears, as well as rocks, Thomas?" Ignatius asked, as his body started to lean slowly forwards. There was a loud squelch and his right rock-leg appeared on the surface. A wave of hydrogen sulphide washed up towards me from the stinking bog. It made me feel a bit sick.

"Bear Grylls is an great adventurer with a very silly name...," I started to explain; but I had to stop explaining quickly, because I could see that if I stayed on Ignatius Bowerman's shoulder, I'd end up soaked in smelly bog slime. I kept one hand on my scarf and, as he leant further forwards into the bog, I crawled carefully around onto his broad rock-back. I hoped, for his sake, that he wasn't going to have to put his face into the green slime. "Keep going, Ignatius, you're doing really well, your right leg is free. You need to start to pull the other leg up now, as though you were going to swim."

"I'd be laughing at what you just said, Thomas, if I didn't think that opening my mouth that much would fill it with fetid bog-slime. We rocks are not exactly well known for our swimming abilities. We have a tendency to ssss..." And with that, Ignatius Bowerman stopped talking. He didn't stop talking because he'd forgotten what he was saying or because he was grumpy; he stopped talking because his rock-face had gone underneath the green bog water. I tried not very hard not to panic at this moment. I was really worried about my rock-friend, but I could see that his left leg was, at last, coming free of the bog. I sat as still as I possibly could on his back, and hoped very hard that a rock that had once been a man could make his way to the edge of the bog without sinking.

In the end, there was one vital thing about Ignatius Bowerman that saved us both from becoming bog-preserved bodies for forensic scientists to dissect. The vital thing was that Ignatius Bowerman was very tall. He was so tall in fact, that as soon as he reached out one of his rock arms, he was able to grab onto a small tree trunk, and start pulling us both towards the edge of the bog. As he did this, I continued to sit as still as I possibly could and shout loud words of encouragement. "Come on Ignatius Bowerman! You can do it! Keep pulling!" I shouted the words loudly because Ignatius Bowerman's rock-ears looked as though they had plugs of slimy grass roots in them.

I think it was more Ignatius Bowerman's determination than my shouting that did it; but eventually, and with a lot of effort, my brave rock-friend pulled us both out of the bog and onto more solid ground. He lay face down for a while and I slid off his back to check that he was okay. He was so big that by lying on the grass, he'd squashed seven gorse bushes, but I could tell that he was fine. I could tell this because he turned his head to look at me and said, "Well, Thomas, is life with you always this exciting?" This question made me smile, because most people would *(and do)* say that the life of a boy whose favourite hobby is looking up information on the internet, is very boring and not at all exciting.

"Not really Ignatius," I said, "it's only been exciting since I've met you."

"Well then, I think we should stick together, young man. A bit of excitement and adventure is good for the soul, and my soul has been in need of cheering up these last years." As he said this, Ignatius Bowerman knelt up. "Now. Shall we go and find my hounds?"

Ignatius Bowerman had said the last thing that he'd said quite seriously; but when I looked at him kneeling on the grass next to me, I had to laugh again, because he had bits of bog-slime hanging off him. It hung from his rock-arms, and sat on his rock-head like a green, smelly wig. "Oh Ignatius," I laughed, "you do look funny, I wish I had a mirror, so I could show you. You have bog slime all over you."

Ignatius Bowerman put his rock-hand up to his rock-head, and felt the green slime that was sitting there. "You know, I think that I used to have hair exactly like this when I was a hunter," he chuckled, pulling the weed off in clumps and looking at it. "Yes indeed, long, green, stinking hair; but that was usually only when I could get out of having a bath!" And then we were both laughing together again, and I was thinking that I was ever so glad that I'd met my unusual friend, because I didn't get to laugh with friends very often, because I didn't have any.

"Come on Ignatius," I said between spurts of laughter, "let's get ourselves up to Bonehill Rocks, and see if your hounds are there." I had to pull some bog slime off my rock-friend's knees and shoulders, before I could climb back up to my usual place. My red scarf wasn't red any more; it was snot-green colour with a few red patches *(people say 'snot green' but snot is actually yellow)*. I didn't mind, but I thought that I should probably hide it from Mum. I wrapped the slimy scarf back around me. "I'm ready Ignatius, let's avoid the bogs this time shall we?"

"I'm definitely going to avoid bogs from now on," replied Ignatius Bowerman, "nasty stinking things. What a horrible way for poor little Bog Dog to die. Now Thomas, which way do we need to go?"

This was a good question. I'd been concentrating so hard on not peeing, peeing and getting out of the bog, that I'd lost my sense of direction. I took the torch out of my fleece pocket and shone it around me; Bell Tor was up behind us on the other side of the bog, I recognised it because it had a steep slope one side and a much flatter one the other side. I knew that Bonehill Rocks were next to a lane, but I didn't know where the lane was. I shone the torch around a bit more, but couldn't see a lane. "There might be another bog," I warned Ignatius Bowerman, "I can see which direction we need to go in, but it'd be better if I could see exactly where the lane is. I know that it's over there somewhere." I pointed with the torch, "If you stand up, I might be able to see it."

"Then I'll stand up, young Thomas," said Ignatius Bowerman. "I want to get to Bonehill Rocks as much as you do. Hold tight." Almost before he'd said, 'Hold tight,' Ignatius Bowerman started moving; and I clung on to his neck, as he heaved himself to his feet. "There you go, Thomas," he said as he turned to face the direction in which I'd been pointing the torch, "Can you see the lane now?"

"I can't see the lane Ignatius," I replied, "But I can see something better than that. I can see Bonehill Rocks."

"You mean those rocks over there?" said my excited rock-friend. "Shall we go there now?" And he started to move forwards.

"Whoa!" I cried. "We have to be careful! Remember the bogs." But my cries were to no avail. *('To no avail' is a phrase that means the same as, 'completely useless').* Like the excellent hunter that he used to be, Ignatius Bowerman had seen his prey *(Bonehill Rocks)* and was hunting it down. Luckily for both of us and for my investigation, Ignatius Bowerman didn't walk into another bog. In fact, it only took four of his giant strides before he was standing on the lane; right next to what I was sure were Bonehill Rocks.

Ignatius Bowerman stood for 43 seconds looking at the rocks and then said, "Oh, no!"

"What's the matter, Ignatius?" I asked.

"I can't see any hounds," he replied. "You said that my hounds would be here on Bonehill Rocks, but none of these rocks look like hounds."

I shone the torch around. He was right; I couldn't see any rocks that looked like hounds, either. There were lots of different-sized rocks, scattered around in no particular pattern; but they were angular, and definitely didn't look at all hound-like.

I didn't like to think that my investigation had let Ignatius Bowerman down so I tried to soothe his concerns, "I didn't say that your hounds were definitely here Ignatius; I said that they might be. I think that we need to do a proper, systematic search, before we decide that they aren't." I know about systematic searches, because forensic scientists have to be systematic when they dissect dead bodies. It means having a system for doing something, instead of doing it in a disorganised way. *(I like systems)*. I knew that a systematic search was a good idea, but there was a problem with it; it was still too dark for me to see Bonehill Rocks properly. I could see the outline of each rock, and I could shine my torch on them if I went close enough, but there were hundreds of rocks spread out across a wide area.

I tried to explain the problem, "I'm really sorry Ignatius, but I'm not sure how to do a systematic search in the dark. I know that you can see in the dark, but I can't and I don't think that you will be very good at being systematic."

I was surprised by Ignatius Bowerman's response. "Oh Thomas, you're being silly again. We don't need to look for my hounds in a systematic way, or in any way at all. If they're here, they'll come when I call them."

I did wonder then, why Ignatius Bowerman hadn't told me before, that the hounds would come when he called them. This would have been very important information for my investigation. I didn't wonder for long though because, by then, I knew how forgetful my rock-friend was, even with important information.

"Are you sure that your hounds will hear you now that they're rocks?" I asked. It seemed like a reasonable question to me, because rocks don't usually have ears.

"There you go with more silliness, Thomas. Of course my hounds will hear me; their ears are finely tuned to my voice."

"But they're rocks now," I argued. "Are you sure that rock-hounds even have ears to hear you with?"

"Thomas, now I think you're just being difficult. I'm certain that my hounds will hear me when I call them. I can hear you, can I not, and I'm a rock?"

I wasn't at all sure about this, and suddenly felt very tired; but I decided that Ignatius Bowerman calling his hounds was probably the best option that we had. It was certainly a better option than spending hours shining a torch at individual rocks, and hoping that one would be a hound.

So I said, "Okay then, go ahead and call them. Is there anything that you need me to do?"

"Yes there is," said Ignatius Bowerman, kneeling down slowly. "I think it would be best if you got off my shoulder. I'm going to use my loudest voice, and it might cause you to fall off."

I thought that it was unlikely that Ignatius Bowerman's voice would make me fall off his shoulder, even though it had once hurt my ears; but I climbed down anyway, because my investigation had disappointed him. "Shall I go and stand on the other side of the lane?" I suggested, "then you won't have to worry about me."

"That would be ideal Thomas. Thank you very much." And with that Ignatius Bowerman turned away from me, and walked towards the top of Bonehill Rocks.

By the time I'd crossed the lane and turned back round to look at him, Ignatius Bowerman was standing very still, right on the top of Bonehill Rocks. Until then he'd mostly seemed misplaced and awkward in his rock form; but as he stood at the top, as still as a rock *(which he was)*, he looked magnificent. For the first time since I'd met him, I could see the hunter that Ignatius Bowerman had once been. It was as though a human-hunter and a towering-rock had been joined together in some magical way *(not that magic is real)*. If Ignatius Bowerman hadn't been my friend *(which he was)* I'd have been scared because, standing there, with the pile of rocks under his feet, he looked as though he'd stamped on a hillside and with one stamp, had sent a wave of broken rocks tumbling down the hill.

(I'd like to point out here, person who is reading my non-story, that the last paragraph looks as though I was using my imagination to write it. I wasn't because I can't do imagining; how I described what

I could see, was exactly how it looked that night, next to Bonehill Rocks in the dark).

When Ignatius Bowerman started shouting, I was very glad that I was on the other side of the lane, and not still on his shoulder. His voice was so loud that the ground shook. *(Those words, 'the ground shook' are sometimes a metaphor, but this time they were not, the ground actually did shake. I could feel it vibrating through my trainers).* If I'd been able to measure it on the Richter Scale, *(which is a scale invented by Mr Richter, that measures the amount of energy released by earthquakes)* I'd have given it number three, which is a small earthquake that people can feel.

I thought Ignatius Bowerman was going to shout the names of his hounds, 'King, Lustleigh, Grim, Bovey, Raven, Hunter and Rocky', but he didn't. Instead he used one single word. It was a simple word; but he made it sound like the long call of a hunting horn. "Hou-ounds! Hou-ounds! Hou-ounds!" he repeated his shout three times with a gap between each. I could tell that in the gaps, he was listening for his hounds.

I didn't do anything while he was shouting, except stand still and hope very, very hard that Ignatius Bowerman's hounds would hear him, and show themselves.

Eleven
Hound Tor

At that moment, *(the moment when Ignatius Bowerman had just shouted three times for his hounds)*; the thing that I absolutely, most of all wanted to happen was to see seven rock-hounds leap out from their hiding place on Bonehill Rocks. After that, there were two other things that I wanted to see; I wanted to see the hounds jump up at Ignatius Bowerman and I wanted to see him bend down to touch their rock-heads. But that's not what I saw, because Ignatius

Bowerman's hounds were not on Bonehill Rocks at all, they were somewhere else. I knew that they were somewhere else for one very good, and very exciting reason; it was such a good and exciting reason, that I'm going to put it in a list all on its own:

1. I could hear Ignatius Bowerman's hounds howling.

I was the most excited that I'd been, not just in my investigation, but ever in my whole life. *(Although I'm not sure about the bit of my life when I was a baby, because I can't remember if I was excited or not then)*.

I hope, person who is reading my non-story, that you're just as excited now, as I was at that moment *(the moment when I heard Ignatius Bowerman's hounds)*. I hope that you are, and I hope that you can cope with just a little bit more excitement. Are you ready? Not only could I hear Ignatius Bowerman's hounds, but I knew exactly where they were. They weren't on Bonehill Rocks they were at Big Tor! Big Tor was the tor just above the car park, where I got on and off my school bus. It wasn't really called Big Tor; I'd given it that name myself and thought that it was a good one, because the tor was indeed quite big. Now though, I had an important investigation reason to find out its real name. I grabbed the map out of my pocket and jabbed my finger onto the right place; I jabbed it so hard that it hurt. When I saw the real name for Big Tor, I made a loud 'whoopee' sound *(which is a very unusual thing for an extra-ordinary boy like me to do)*. I made the sound because the name fitted perfectly, Hound Tor! Of course, hounds would be at Hound Tor, it was obvious when I saw the name, and I didn't know *(and I still don't know now)* why my map investigation hadn't made me see it before then.

I turned around to tell Ignatius Bowerman the good news, but he wasn't at the top of Bonehill Rocks any longer; he was at the bottom and he was about to walk right past me in the direction of Hound *(Big)* Tor.

"Ignatius! Wait, wait for me!" I shouted. "I've some marvellous news to tell you."

"I know what your news is Thomas," Ignatius Bowerman replied. I could hear emotion in his rock-voice. "I heard my hounds and I'm going to see them! I'm going to see them for the first time in three hundred years! Are you coming?"

It was clear that this was another rhetorical question because, as he said, 'Are you coming?' Ignatius Bowerman bent down, picked me up and put me under his rock-arm; like he had the first time he'd carried me. Then he started running.

You people, who can imagine, can probably imagine what it felt like being carried in that way by a running rock. I'm convinced *(and I must go back and investigate soon)* that the thuds of my rock-friend's feet as he ran must have made indents in the ground. I'm also convinced that a rock as big as Ignatius Bowerman running across Dartmoor must have caused the same ground to shake, even more than it had when he was shouting. It was such a jarring, muddling experience that I can't really tell you much about the short trip across to Hound *(Big)* Tor. I didn't like it, but I was so happy and excited for my rock-friend, that I didn't mind being jarred and muddled, I didn't mind at all!

When we got to Hound Tor car park *(I have decided to stop calling it 'Big Tor' now)*. Ignatius Bowerman put me down, well, he didn't exactly put me down, it was more like he dropped me. It hurt when I landed on my bottom, but I was soon on my feet again. Not soon enough though, to allow me to keep up with Ignatius Bowerman, who had crossed the road and was striding up the hill towards the rocks. I set off running after him, but had to stop about half way up *(I have told you before that I'm really bad at running)*. It was starting to get dimpsy *(a bit light and a bit dark)* by now, and I could clearly see the outline of the rocks above me.

Because I'd spent a lot of time looking at the tor while I waited for my school bus *(the ordinary students who go on the school bus don't want to talk to me and I don't want to talk to them)*, I thought that I knew the line and shape of the rocks really well. But as I stood panting and looking at them that night, it was obvious, really, really obvious, to me that the rocks were not just rock-shaped, they were also hound-shaped!

Ignatius Bowerman was at the top now, standing on the flat, grassy plateau between the two sets of rocks. He called his hounds again, not as loud as he had over on Bonehill Rocks, but more gently, as if he was trying to persuade them to come out. And as Ignatius Bowerman called, I saw something marvellous happening.

I know, person who is reading my non-story, that I've told you some unbelievable things so far. Talking rocks, witches and boys who can't imagine, may all be unbelievable to you. But, if you're going to believe just one thing that I tell you *(and this really, really is a non-story)* please believe that as I stood there, half way up to Hound Tor, I saw rocks that were a bit hound-shaped, turn into hounds that were a bit rock-shaped. First they started to move, a leg here, a tail there; and then the jagged lines of the rocks started to smooth out. Heads appeared, and lifted and looked around. They knew what they were looking for, and I knew what they were looking for. They were looking for their master, the famous hunter Ignatius Bowerman.

It didn't take them long to find him. He called to them, he reached his rock-hands out towards them and they went to him. I'm not going to describe the scene that I saw next. I know that you want me to, but I'm not going to. I'm not going to for three reasons:

1. I'm not good at describing.
2. It was a private meeting between a man and his long-lost best friends.
3. My mum told me that saying no words is sometimes better than saying lots of words.

After four minutes of watching the scene that I'm not going to describe, I walked up the rest of the hill towards Ignatius Bowerman and his hounds. My rock-friend looked so happy, that I felt happy too. I felt happy enough, in fact, to hug his rock-leg when I got to him *(I have already told you that I don't like hugging)*.

"Ah, Thomas, my very good friend, there you are. Allow me the complete and utter pleasure of introducing you to my hounds; this is King, first at every kill, these two are Grim and Lustleigh, this old pair of codgers are Bovey and Raven, and this fat greedy guts is Hunter."

I'd like to be able to tell you what Ignatius Bowerman's hounds looked like, but I can't because they were all rushing around him in circles, jumping up at him and licking his rock-hands. Instead of six hounds with six tails and twenty-four paws, I could see one big, circling hound with six tails and twenty-four paws. Because this big, circling hound also had six heads, which had six jaws with six sets of sharp hunting teeth, I stood back, it didn't seem like a good time to tell Ignatius Bowerman that I was a bit scared of his hounds, so I stood and watched the scene in front of me.

I must have done some counting while I was watching *(I sometimes do counting without realising that I'm doing it)* because I had a moment of sudden realisation. *(A moment of sudden realisation is exactly what it sounds like it is).* My realisation was this, *'Ignatius Bowerman had seven hounds, there were only six hounds there on Hound Tor, one of his hounds was missing, and the hound that was missing was Rocky'.* I didn't know what to do about Rocky, Ignatius Bowerman seemed so happy, it would have been mean to spoil his enjoyment by telling him some bad news. So I sat down on a rock *(one that wasn't a hound and wasn't moving or talking)* and watched Ignatius Bowerman petting his hounds.

After an hour of sitting on a rock two things were happening:

1. I was starting to get very cold.
2. It was starting to get properly light.

I wasn't too worried about getting very cold, friends are important, and if you have to get very cold while a friend greets his long lost hounds, then you should just do it. But I was worried about the daylight. Hound Tor was very near to a road, a car park and two houses. I didn't know how early the people in the houses would wake up, but I did know that if people did wake up or drive past, they were going to be very shocked if they saw the rock called 'Bowerman's Nose' at Hound Tor, and the rocks that were supposed to be at Hound Tor, running around like actual hounds. I checked my adventure watch with the camouflage strap; it was five minutes to four and it was time for me to do something about the hound-slash-tor-slash-talking-rock situation. I walked over to Ignatius Bowerman and his rampant hounds. *(Rampant can mean uncontrolled which the hounds looked but weren't. It can also mean 'standing up on back legs' which is exactly what they were doing).*

I stood two metres away *(which felt very close to the hounds indeed)* and shouted up at Ignatius Bowerman. "Excuse me. Excuse me, Ignatius, I've something important to say."

"Ah, young Thomas, I wondered where you'd got to. Have you met my hounds?" My rock-friend replied, grinning, but looking at his hounds and not at me.

He'd forgotten something again, but it didn't matter. "I've met your hounds and they're ...

they're..." I struggled to find a word because I thought that the hounds were 'enormous', 'terrifying' and 'evil-looking'. Those were obviously words I couldn't tell Ignatius Bowerman because his hounds were his favourite things. "... They're freaky." I chose the word 'freaky' for two reasons:

1. It is a word that the boys at school sometimes use about me, when they look a bit scared of my cleverness.
2. Rocks that are actually hounds are extremely unusual, and 'freaky' can mean 'extremely unusual' if you want it to.

"I've never heard that word before, Thomas," replied Ignatius Bowerman, "but I can only assume that it's a compliment, because my hounds are so magnificent that compliments are inevitable. Please allow me to return the compliment, and say that you're a very fine investigator, who should be awarded a prize for investigation. Do they have prizes like that at your school?"

"Thank you, Ignatius," I said, stepping back

another pace to avoid Hunter's paws *(I think it was Hunter)*. "But I already know I'm a very fine investigator, because my investigations helped to find your hounds. I don't think there is a school prize for investigating, but I do know that there is a school prize for story-telling."

"Well then, you should write this story, the story of Ignatius Bowerman, the magnificent hunter who lost his hounds, and Thomas, the intelligent investigator who found them. People would like to read such a story, I'm sure."

"I'd really like to write this story, Ignatius," I said so quietly that, with his hounds still rushing around, I didn't think Ignatius Bowerman would hear me. "I'd really like to, but I can't write stories because I can't do imagining."

It was obvious that my rock-friend had heard me then because he looked at me and then settled his hounds down so that they were lying at his feet. I'd like to be able to tell you how he did this, but I can't. I can't tell you, because I don't know. It may have been a rock-hand gesture or a word that I didn't hear, or maybe a hunter's relationship with his hounds is so close, they just know what he wants them to do. Whichever it was, the six hounds lay down in a circle around their rock-master, looking up at him.

"I think you should write this story, Thomas," my rock-friend Ignatius Bowerman said using a quiet rock voice, "you won't need to use your imagination, because you've seen everything that happened in it. It's a story that should be told, and I'd like you to tell it."

"I'll think about what you've said, Ignatius," I replied, feeling a strange warmth in my cheeks, "but for now, we have two more important things to think about:

1. It is getting light; you're not on Hayne Down, and your hounds are not rocks.
2. We haven't found Rocky, your seventh hound."

"Ah, Rocky. My good and loyal friend," said Ignatius Bowerman, "how kind of you to worry about him, Thomas, but you didn't need to. I must also be a good investigator, because I've worked out exactly where Rocky is."

"Where is he, Ignatius?" I asked, "is he hiding somewhere here on Hound Tor?"

Ignatius Bowerman laughed a gentle laugh. "No, Thomas, Rocky isn't here. I'll show you where he is later; but for now, you're right, I need to get my hounds back into their places, and I need to return to Hayne Down."

And with that *(which actually means 'just after that')* Ignatius Bowerman stooped down and whispered something into Raven's ear. At least I think it was Raven, because he his ears were ragged around the edges like Dog's had been before he died; it might have been Bovey because there were two hounds with ragged ears and Ignatius Bowerman had said that they were both old. Raven *(or Bovey)* licked his master's face, stood up and walked slowly up to the rock that he'd come from. He settled himself down in his place with his old eyes staring at Ignatius Bowerman. As he settled down and became still, his curves became more angular, and his tail tucked itself underneath him; soon Raven *(or Bovey)* was a rock again. One by one, Ignatius

Bowerman said goodbye to his hounds, and one by one, they took their places on Hound Tor.

When the last one had gone, he turned to me and said, "Well, Thomas, this old and forgetful rock can't thank you enough for the great service you've done me. I've seen my hounds again, and I'm content."

"But Ignatius, now that you know where they are, you can come and see them any night that you want to," I replied, not understanding what Ignatius was trying to tell me.

"I could," said my rock-friend gazing at the shapes on Hound Tor, "But I'm a forgetful rock, and there's no guarantee I'll be able to remember where they are."

"I'll help you Ignatius," I tried to reassure him. "I'll help you every night, if you want me to."

Ignatius Bowerman looked down at me "Thank you, Thomas, I know you will. But you're a boy, and boys grow up. I knew a girl once that grew up, you remind me of her. One day, you'll have your own investigation to undertake; your investigation into life and all of its adventures. When that happens, you'll be too busy to remember me."

This seemed like a very sad thing for my rock-friend to say, but there was a chance it was true. I wasn't a grown-up, so I didn't know what grown-ups did and didn't remember.

So I didn't say what ordinary people usually say in stories, which is "I'll never forget you, Ignatius." Instead, I said a thing that an extra-ordinary boy called Thomas might say. I said, "It's getting light, Ignatius, it's time for us to go back to Hayne Down."

The trip back to Hayne Down was such a short one, that I didn't ride on Ignatius Bowerman's shoulder. Instead, we walked, cold boy-hand in cold rock-hand, down the road to my lane. I opened the gate *(because that's my job)* and we walked through it together *(I shut the gate again, because that's the Countryside Code)*. I thought briefly about what the boys at school might say if they saw me holding hands with a rock-man. They would probably call me 'weird' and 'freak' and 'gay'; but I didn't think about this for very long, they're not my friends, and friends are what's important.

When we got to the end of my drive, I stood in front of Ignatius Bowerman, looked up at him and said, "It has been a great investigation, Ignatius, I'll see you again soon."

Ignatius Bowerman smiled and looked down at me. Then he chuckled. "At last Thomas! At last you have forgotten something that I've remembered. Maybe you're the forgetful one, after all."

"I'm not forgetful Ignatius," I replied, smiling, "I'm just very, very tired. What is it that I've forgotten, and you've remembered?"

Ignatius Bowerman didn't answer my question then. In fact, he didn't answer it at all. What he did do was turn around to face where he usually stood and call quietly up the hill. "Ro-cky, Ro-cky, Ro-cky."

I realised what I'd forgotten then, and I smiled because I almost never forget things. I'd forgotten about Rocky; could it be that he'd been with Ignatius Bowerman on Hayne Down all of the time? It was light enough to see up the hill now, and the largest boulder that was usually at Ignatius Bowerman's feet, the one that I'd sat on to talk to him, was moving. It was moving, and it was changing shape. It was moving and it was changing shape and it was running down the hill towards Ignatius Bowerman and towards me.

"I worked it out, Thomas," said Ignatius Bowerman. "I worked it out. Rocky was always loyal, he never left my side and he slept on my bed. Where else would he be now he's a rock, but right here with me on Hayne Down?"

Ignatius Bowerman's question was a rhetorical one. So I didn't answer it. Ignatius Bowerman was silent too, and with one last gentle pat on my head, he turned around and strode up his hill to meet Rocky, his very loyal hound.

I turned around too and walked slowly down my drive. I knew that behind me there would be a tall man-slash-rock and a short hound-slash-rock who would be overjoyed to see each other *(I'm not sure what could be better than joy, but it must be really good)*. When I got to our front porch, I hesitated, and then I turned slowly around.

There was nothing unusual to see; at least, there would have been nothing unusual for an ordinary person to see; an ordinary person who hadn't just been doing an investigation with a rock-friend named Ignatius Bowerman, his rock-brother named Figgie Daniel and his rock-hounds named Grim, Hunter, Raven, Bovey, Lustleigh, King and Rocky.

But I saw plenty, because my name is Thomas, I'm eleven years, six months and fourteen days old and I'm extra-ordinary.

Epilogue

An epilogue is the end bit of a story, that tells you something extra. This is a non-story, but I still want to tell you something extra. Here's a conversation that I had with my Mum one rainy night, a year and two days after I'd finished my investigation with Ignatius Bowerman.

Me: *Mum, do you know that the tall rock opposite our house is called Bowerman's Nose?*

Mum: *Yes I do, at least, that's what most people call him.*

Me: *You said 'him' then, I say 'him' too. Do you call him a different name to most people?*

Mum: *I've my own name for him, yes. I learnt it when I was a girl visiting my grandparents.*

Me: *Do you also know that the tor next to the bus car park is called Hound Tor?*

Mum: *Yes, Thomas, and I know the reason for that name. I also know that what is hidden there, is sometimes forgotten.*

Me: *Do you believe that strange things can happen, even to extra-ordinary boys who can't do imagining?*

Mum: *I believe that strange things happen to all sorts of people, all the time.*

Me: *You know about Ignatius Bowerman, don't you?*

Mum: *Yes, my precious extra-ordinary boy, I do. I met him when I was a girl and I helped him to find his hounds on Hound Tor.*

There was a gap in the conversation then while I thought about what my Mum had said *(Mrs Aitken told me that a 'gap in the conversation' means a little bit of silence)*. I thought about that, and about the things Mum had said when she noticed me creeping out of the house, and about the map, and the torch I didn't know was in my drawer. There were so many questions to ask, but it didn't feel right to ask any of them apart from this one.

Me: *Why didn't you tell me that you knew where the hounds were?*

Mum: *Because Thomas, the best lives, even extra-ordinary ones, are full of stories and everyone should write at least one story in their lifetime.*

So I did, and you have just read it.

Now you have read my non-story you probably want to go to Dartmoor and meet Ignatius Bowerman, his hounds and his annoying brother Figgie Daniel; or you might want to stay on your sofa and watch loud television instead; I don't know because I don't know you.

You could do some internet research to find the right places on Dartmoor, or you could look at this list. If you have read my non-story properly, you will know that the numbers are grid references for a map. The map you need to buy *(or ask your mum to buy)* is called OL28; it is orange and made by a company called Ordnance Survey who are very clever and know how tall hills are and which way north is.

If you go to Dartmoor *(but not if you stay on your sofa and watch loud television)* don't be surprised if you see strange things. My mum once said, 'Strange things happen to all sorts of people, all the time.' She was a bit right.

Ignatius Bowerman
(Bowerman's Nose)   741 804
Daniel Bowerman
(Figgie Daniel)   734 822
Natsworthy Manor
(Natwsorthy Manor) 721 799
Bonehill Rocks
(Bonehill Rocks)   731 774
Big Tor
(Hound Tor)   742 790

Who is Fi?

Fi Darby is the co-author of the popular Dartmoor blog Two Blondes Walking.

The Two Blondes love Dartmoor, their families and Jelly Babies.

They spend much of their spare time teaching and leading young people on Dartmoor and are proud to be involved in both the Ten Tors Challenge and the Duke of Edinburgh's Award.

The Two Blondes are also Ordnance Survey 'Get Outside' Champions. They were chosen for this role in recognition of their love of the outdoors and their ability to communicate that love to other people.

With special thanks to Ordnance Survey for their kind provision of the contour images used in this book. Those of you who love maps and Dartmoor as much as we do might recognise some familiar features.

Also by Fi Darby and the Two Blondes.

The Dartmoor Christmas Tree

Tree lives on his own, high up on Dartmoor. Tree loves the moor, but starts to feel sad when unkind Buzzard teases him about his travels and the sights that he has seen. It takes some special Christmas visitors to show Tree just how excellent and important he really is.

Dart the River

Dart is a river. He starts life in a bog high on Dartmoor. This book tells the story of Dart's adventures, as he splashes his way down off Dartmoor to the sea at Dartmouth. A 'Find and Explore' book from Two Blondes Walking. Read the story then visit the locations for yourself.